KILLER PURSUIT

Whisper Island Mystery Series -2

Jenny Elaine

PROLOGUE

Azalea – 1966

The old grandfather clock echoed loudly throughout the house, and I stopped writing to count the chimes. It was nine o'clock; I was supposed to be gone already. With a sigh, I looked back at the letter I was writing, the words blurring before my eyes. I'd been at it for over an hour, and I was exhausted. I couldn't, however, stop now. There was still more to write. If something happened to me, I wanted my family to know the truth.

I could hear the wind whistling through the trees outside, and I got up to look out the window. A hurricane was heading our way, and it had been raining off and on for the last several hours. Right now, however, not a drop fell from the sky. The only evidence of the approaching storm was the steadily increasing strength of the wind. I could see how it shook the oak tree right outside my window and I shivered; storms always made me feel both a little edgy and excited. Tonight was different, though. Tonight, I felt something ominous approaching, and I feared the storm wasn't the only threat I would soon face.

Shaking my head, as if to clear the jumbled thoughts that bounced madly about, I sat down and began to write again. Twenty minutes later, I finally finished. I quickly folded the pages together, placed them in an envelope, and went to hide my secret. Ten minutes later, I had just finished packing when, suddenly, a loud creak downstairs caused me to catch my breath. I waited, listening as my heart began to race.

There it was again, only closer this time. Someone was in the house, and I knew they were searching for me.

Rushing over to my writing desk, I jotted down one last sentence in my diary before slamming it closed and placing it back into the secret compartment. I didn't want anyone to find that book until I was certain this really was the end. I quickly locked the desk and slipped the chain with the key around my neck.

Realizing I didn't have much time, I flipped off the lights and ran to my bedroom door, peering out into the dark hallway. I didn't see anyone, and so I tiptoed out, standing completely still as I listened.

Tap, tap, tap.

Someone was coming up the stairs.

Legs trembling, I went back into my room and hurried over to the window. *If I can make it to the carriage house, I'll take the car and get out of here,* I told myself as I opened the window and slipped out onto the roof. I pushed the window back down and carefully made my way toward the grand old oak. I'd slipped out this way so many times as a teenager that I could almost do it with my eyes closed. Tonight, however, was proving to be more difficult as the wind caused my steps to falter. I slipped, and for one breathtaking moment, I feared I would fall off the roof. I was barely able to catch myself, and with a deep breath, I continued toward the tree.

Leaves rustled as I threw a leg over one of the massive branches and made my way down the old oak. The night was black, as heavy clouds filled the sky, and the air was humid. Suddenly, a lone owl screeched loudly in the distance and I jerked in surprise, nearly losing my grip on the tree. The eerie sound sent chills down my spine, and I wondered if it could possibly be a bad omen.

Finally, I reached the bottom. Just when I touched my feet to the ground, I saw my bedroom light click on. I froze, making certain to stay hidden beneath the oak's shadows.

I peered up through the leaves and branches, my breath catching when I spotted a dark silhouette standing at my window. It stood there, so still and ominous that I wondered if I really wasn't hidden after all. I could almost feel those piercing eyes staring right at me. After a moment, the shadow moved away, and I blew out a sigh of relief as I raised a trembling hand to push a lock of fiery auburn hair out of my eyes. Taking a deep breath, I raced around the side of the house in the direction of the carriage house.

As soon as I reached the back of the house, I paused, my chest heaving. Looking around, I rubbed my arms, trying to ward off the feeling of foreboding. Giant oak trees towered overhead, and the Spanish moss that hung from their branches blew lifelessly back and forth in the breeze like silver ghosts. I didn't see anyone, but something about the way the shadows of the trees moved along the ground made me feel like I was being watched. Glancing upward, I saw no more lights in the upstairs windows and knew I needed to hurry.

Stepping away from the comforting shadow of the house, I hurried across the yard. Finally, I made it to the carriage house, and with a sigh of relief, I slid the huge door open and stepped inside. Suddenly, a loud scream sounded in the darkness, and something furry brushed against my leg. With a gasp, I stumbled backward, crashing into the door as a cat shot off across the yard, disappearing among the bushes.

Shaking all over, I flipped on the light and raced to my car, my heart pounding so hard I feared I might faint. I'd just opened the driver's side door when a figure stepped into the doorway of the carriage house and a voice said, "Going somewhere?"

At exactly the same moment, the clouds released their burden, and a massive sheet of rain gushed from the heavens.

CHAPTER 1

Present Day

Z aylie Layne could hardly believe her eyes. The skeletal remains of a human body had just been unearthed in her backyard, and if she was correct in her assumption, those bones belonged to her great aunt, Azalea Layne.

"I'll go call the police," Gran said, her voice trembling as she turned to hurry into the house.

"I-I've never seen a real skeleton before."

Zaylie turned to look at her best friend, Rita Steele, who stood at her side with a death grip on her arm. Her face had turned pale, and by the way she was swaying on her feet, Zaylie feared she might faint.

"Why don't you go inside with Gran and sit down?" Zaylie asked. "You don't look too good."

"I don't feel too good either," Rita replied, covering her mouth.

The construction supervisor, Alan Whitlock, waved to Zaylie as he walked their way. He'd gone to school with her parents and had lived on the island for as long as Zaylie could remember.

"Miss Layne, one of my men found this near the body," Alan said as he held out his hand to reveal an old key hanging from a silver chain. "I told him he should have left it alone, but he said he found it right before he found the body."

Zaylie took the key and studied it with a furrowed brow. Looking back at Mr. Whitlock, she asked, "Didn't Gran say this area used to be where the old garage was located?"

Alan wiped his sweaty brow and nodded. "Yes, ma'am, but I believe they called it a carriage house back then," he replied. "I remember when your mom and dad tore it down and added the garage to the house." Glancing uncertainly at Rita, he asked, "Miss Steele, are you okay? You don't look so good."

The color swiftly returned to Rita's cheeks at his comment, but before she could respond, one of the workers beckoned to Mr. Whitlock. As he walked away, Rita put her hands on her hips and stated, "I wish people would quit telling me how awful I look. It's not every day I see a dead body, you know!" Turning to look back at the skeleton, she sighed and added, "So much for getting your new training center built, Zaylie. If I know old Sheriff Carter, he'll insist on investigating for months just to be annoying."

"Of all times for Uncle Bill to have gallbladder surgery," Zaylie muttered.

Bill Harper wasn't her real uncle, but he was like family to her. As sheriff of Whisper Island, he'd worked relentlessly to help track down her sister's killer and had become a very dear friend in the process. He wouldn't, however, be able to take back over as sheriff for another few weeks until he'd healed from his surgery. Odin Carter had agreed to come out of retirement and take back over until Uncle Bill recovered, but Zaylie wished the town had hired someone else instead.

As Zaylie continued to study the key in her hand, she asked, "What do you think this goes to?"

"Maybe an old treasure chest," Rita suggested, wiggling her eyebrows.

Moments later, the police arrived, and everyone was ordered to clear the area. As they stepped back to watch, Zaylie noticed Gran wiping a tear from her eye.

Wrapping a supportive arm around her shoulders, Zaylie said, "I'm sorry, Gran. I know this is hard for you."

Gran and Azalea Layne had grown up together and were once the best of friends. In some ways, they were almost like sisters. Zaylie never knew the circumstances surrounding Azalea's strange disappearance over fifty years ago, but she intended to find out.

Sheriff Carter, who was in his late 70s, questioned everyone while the other officers investigated the crime scene. Before his retirement, he'd been the sheriff of Whisper Island for nearly forty years. He was a few years older than Gran, and the two had never gotten along.

"If that really is Azalea Layne's body," he said to Gran, "I'm certain it was her partner who killed her."

With flashing eyes, Gran snapped, "She didn't have a partner, Odin. I know you always thought she was involved in that robbery and shooting, but there was never any actual proof against her."

His thin lips pursing in irritation, he stated, "The police found her standing over the dead guard's body, Louella. You can't deny the facts."

"The guard was also in love with her," Gran returned, her cheeks growing redder by the minute. "She told you that he'd sent her a note to meet him at the bank the night of the robbery."

"What robbery?" Zaylie interjected, looking between the two of them. "What are you talking about?"

Looking a little snide, Sheriff Carter said, "I guess the family has done a good job of keeping the whole sordid story undercover. Isn't that right, Louella?"

By the stormy look on Gran's face, Zaylie was afraid she was about to have to break up a fight. Taking her grandmother's arm, she said, "Let's go inside, Gran, where we can talk privately."

"I'll let you know if I have any more questions," Sheriff Carter called out as the two women stalked away.

"Oh, the nerve of that man," Gran fumed as they walked up the back porch steps. "I have never liked him."

"He always has been the disagreeable sort," Zaylie replied.

They stepped into the cool kitchen and closed

the door, but instead of taking a seat, Gran stood at the back window to stare out at the scene unfolding in their backyard. Zaylie moved to stand beside her, shaking her head as she watched Rita flirt with the men on the construction crew.

Looking over at her grandmother, Zaylie asked softly, "Will you tell me what happened, Gran?"

Gran took off her glasses and rubbed her eyes. "Like Odin said, there was a robbery at the bank," she began.

"The bank that was owned by my great-grandfather?" Zaylie asked. "Azalea's and Granddad Joseph's father?"

Gran nodded. "Yes," she replied, replacing the glasses. "He and two other men co-owned the place; it was very successful during its day."

"Why didn't Granddad Joseph ever tell me about that?" Zaylie wondered out loud.

With a sigh, Gran walked over to the kitchen table and sat down. "Because it closed after everything that happened, and no one really cared to talk about it. There were and still are a lot of bad memories surrounding that bank."

Joining Gran at the table, Zaylie said, "I'm listening."

Gran gazed out of the large bay window by the table for a moment, her expression troubled. Finally, she said, "When Azalea and I were about eighteen, the bank was robbed and the guard that she was planning to elope with that night was shot and killed. His name was Russell; Azalea was devastated."

"How awful," Zaylie murmured. "Was a lot of money taken?"

Gran shook her head. "There was no money taken at all. Your great-grandfather and his partners would store jewelry and other valuables that belonged to some of their wealthiest clients at the bank. That night, when the vault was opened, a very valuable diamond set that was going to be given as a gift to Harold Beecher's wife was stolen."

"Harold Beecher?" Zaylie asked.

Gran nodded. "He was one of the partners."

Thinking it all over for a moment, Zaylie finally said, "You said the vault was 'opened' like the thief knew the combination."

Looking at her granddaughter, Gran said, "Yes, because that's exactly what happened. There was no evidence of forced entry at all."

"Wow," Zaylie muttered. Studying her grandmother for a moment, she finally asked in a soft voice, "Why have I never heard about any of this?"

Gran heaved a sigh. "You have to understand, honey, how hard it was back then, and how hard it is for me to talk about it even now," she replied. "Azalea was like a sister to me, and watching the whole town turn against her was awful. After she disappeared, none of us liked talking about it. I think it was easier for all of us to try to bury the past and move on."

A knock sounded at the back door just then,

interrupting their conversation, and Zaylie stood up to let Sheriff Carter in. He stepped into the kitchen, his faded blue eyes landing on Gran as he stated in a monotone voice, "There's a bullet lodged in the spine. We'll have to confirm it's her first, but it looks like Azalea Layne was murdered."

CHAPTER 2

Zaylie

When Shawn Eaton arrived at Azalea Bluff, he was surprised to see police cars lining the driveway. He was the property caretaker, and he came out twice a week to tend the grounds. He'd known that the construction for Zaylie's new training center would be underway out back, so he'd planned to work on the shrubs around the front of the house today. Unable to control his curiosity, he went around back and asked what was going on.

"A body was found," Alan Whitlock explained as he and his men loaded up their equipment.

Shawn had known Alan his whole life and considered the man to be a friend. In his early fifties, Alan was a good fifteen years older than Shawn, but he looked like a man of only forty and had the energy of a teenager.

"Do they have any idea who the body belongs to?" Shawn asked, although he already had a pretty good idea.

Looking around, Alan said in a low voice, "Sheriff Carter thinks it's Azalea Layne," he replied. "Looks like she was murdered."

Shawn raised his eyebrows. "That's a bit of a surprise, isn't it?" he asked. "From what I've heard, most everyone thought she ran off with those diamonds."

Alan shrugged. "It doesn't really surprise me," he replied.

Before Shawn could ask what he meant, Alan shouted out an order to one of his men who was about to back a piece of equipment into a tree. As he hurried over to help guide the driver, Shawn walked back around the house to his car. When he got inside, he locked the doors and pulled out his cell phone, quickly dialing a familiar number.

"Hello?" a voice answered.

"We've got to talk," Shawn stated. "They just found Azalea Layne's body."

Zaylie could hardly believe what Sheriff Carter had just told them. All these years, her great aunt, the beautiful woman from the portrait in the living room, had been buried in their backyard with a bullet in her back?

"Someone shot her?" Gran gasped, her eyes once again filling with tears.

"It looks that way," Odin replied. "We've thoroughly swept the area, but I'm leaving the tape up for now. Please make sure the area stays clear until I say different." Looking at Zaylie, he added, "That goes for your dog, too. I don't want her nosing around and contaminating possible evidence."

Zaylie bristled at his authoritative tone. "Smutti never goes where she doesn't belong, Sheriff."

With a raised eyebrow, he said, "See that she doesn't."

As he walked back outside and shut the door behind him, Zaylie crossed her arms and muttered, "I really don't like that man."

"I just *thought* he was a pain when we were young," Gran fumed. "He really knows how to try one's patience."

Zaylie nodded in agreement. As she went over to the fridge to fix herself a glass of sweet tea, the back door flew open and Rita breezed inside.

"The foreman is so dreamy, don't y'all think?" she asked with a beaming smile. Seeing the expressions on Zaylie and Gran's faces, the smile melted away and she added sheepishly, "Sorry. Bad timing. What did Sheriff Carter say?"

"What did he *not* say?" Zaylie huffed.

"Azalea, if it really is her, was shot," Gran stated.

Rita's eyes widened. "I was so preoccupied with Grady that I didn't hear the police say anything about that," she said in a breathless tone. "Who do you think shot her, Gran?"

Gran shook her head and shrugged. "I have no idea," she replied. Sitting down at the table once again, she rubbed her forehead and murmured, "I can't believe this is happening."

Walking over to the counter, Rita grabbed a cookie from the cookie jar and said, "Grady told me that Mr. Whitlock's dad did some work on this house right before Azalea disappeared."

Zaylie looked at Rita in surprise. "Really? Is he still alive?"

"Yes, he is," Gran spoke up. "You don't know him, Zaylie. He had a stroke years ago and became a recluse."

"Do you think he would mind if we paid him a visit?" Zaylie asked curiously. "Who knows, he might remember something."

Gran shrugged. "I don't know if he would agree to see us or not. We should probably let the police handle it, though, honey."

Rita cocked an eyebrow and asked, "Like they did before? Grady said Azalea was accused of stealing some diamonds and killing the guard, who also happened to be her fiancé. He said the case was never solved."

With a frown, Gran looked at Rita and asked, "Just how does this Grady fellow know so much about a 54-year-old case?"

"His great-uncle was the guard who was killed," Rita replied.

Gran's eyes widened, and she sat back against her chair in shock. "I thought all the Madisons left the island years ago," she breathed.

"The guard's last name was Madison?" Zaylie asked.

"Yes." Gran nodded. "After Russell was killed, his family left Whisper Island, and we never saw them again. I had no idea a member of the family had moved back."

"He moved here about six months ago," Rita told her. "His last name isn't Madison, though; it's Young."

"You got *all* that information in just one conversation?" Zaylie asked her friend incredulously. "Did you also find out his social security number?"

"Maybe," Rita retorted, her black eyes twinkling. "He's awfully good-looking, I know that much."

Zaylie rolled her eyes. "What about Kaleb Bates?" she wanted to know.

Rita waved a hand in the air. "He's been busy taking care of his sick mother," she replied. "We still talk, but most of his time is occupied with seeing about her."

"I've spoken to Grady a couple of times when I've seen him around town," Gran interrupted, referring back to the subject at hand. "I wonder why he never mentioned his connection to Russell?"

Shrugging, Rita said, "Who knows?" Looking at the clock that hung over the stove, her eyes flew open wide and she gasped, "Oh my goodness, I have an appointment at the salon to get to! Keep me posted, y'all."

Nodding, Zaylie waved goodbye as her friend raced from the kitchen. She then went over to the back window and watched as the officers finished putting up the police tape, her mind whirling. Slipping her hand into her skirt pocket, her fingers brushed against a piece of cool metal, and she suddenly remembered the chain and key one of the men had found.

"Gran, do you know what this key could be for?" she asked, pulling it from her pocket.

Gran took the key and studied it for a moment. "It almost looks like the key to the writing desk in your room," she finally replied. "I haven't seen it in years, though. Where did you find it?"

After explaining, Zaylie asked, "Should I run outside and give it to Sheriff Carter before he leaves?"

Shaking her head, Gran stood up and headed toward the front of the house. "Let's see if it fits that desk first."

Zaylie followed Gran upstairs and into her bedroom. Smutti was sitting at the window and turned to look at them when they opened the door. Her smut black coat glistened in the afternoon sun and her golden eyes watched the women closely as they walked across the room toward the antique desk.

"This desk once belonged to Azalea," Gran explained. "Your Grandad Joseph had to pry it open after she died because it was locked shut."

Zaylie stood back and watched as Gran closed the lid on the writing desk and inserted the small key into the lock. It fit perfectly, and after jiggling the rusty key inside the old lock, it turned and clicked.

"You were right, Gran," Zaylie said excitedly.

"Why do you think Azalea locked it the night she died and had the key on a chain around her neck?"

Staring at the old desk with a puzzled expression, Gran said, "It seems she would have locked something important inside, but to my knowledge, nothing was ever found."

"Granddad Joseph wouldn't have taken it and not told anyone, would he?" Zaylie asked.

Gran shook her head. "No, I don't believe so."

Unlocking the desk once again, Gran took a step back and studied the old piece of furniture. Zaylie did the same, her eyes taking in the little nooks and crannies inside. She stepped forward and opened one of the drawers, her brow furrowing when she noticed it wasn't as deep on the inside as it appeared to be on the outside.

"You don't suppose..." she muttered as she gently pressed on the bottom of the drawer.

Suddenly, the bottom moved, and Zaylie could see there was a hidden compartment underneath. She'd always heard that many antique desks had hidden compartments, but she never would have guessed that one existed inside her very own bedroom. Quickly removing the false bottom, Zaylie saw what appeared to be a leather-bound book resting inside.

"Gran, look!" she gasped, pulling the book out for her grandmother to see.

Gran's eyes widened, and she took the book from Zaylie and carefully opened the front cover.

"Zaylie," she said in almost a whisper, "we just

found Azalea's diary."

CHAPTER 3

Zaylie

R eeling from shock and excitement, Zaylie said, "What are we waiting for? Let's read it!"

Zaylie, Gran, and Smutti all hurried downstairs and into the kitchen. Putting on her glasses, Gran turned to the first page and said with a moan, "Oh, dear, the writing is too small and faded for my old eyes. Here, you try."

Taking the book, Zaylie studied the tiny handwriting and said, "This may take longer than we thought, Gran. Her handwriting is like yours; cursive and sloppy."

Bristling, Gran retorted, "My handwriting is *not* sloppy."

Zaylie looked up at her grandmother and cocked an eyebrow. "Your last letter was returned because they couldn't read the address," she stated dryly.

"I can't help it if people can't read cursive writing these days," Gran replied with a sniff.

Not bothering to argue further, Zaylie held the open book up to the light and began to read.

October 2nd, 1966

I decided to start a diary because I needed a way to sort through my jumbled thoughts. Everything is off-kilter right now; it's as if the world has turned upside down. I feel like my whole life is spinning out of control, and I don't know how to make it stop. I've been accused of robbing my father's bank and killing my fiancé...my dearest Russell, how can you be dead? We had so many plans.

Before Zaylie could read any further, her phone suddenly began to ring. With a frustrated huff, she closed the book and grabbed her phone. Bill Harper's name was flashing across the screen, and she immediately answered and put the call on speakerphone.

"Hi, Uncle Bill," she greeted the old family friend. "How are you feeling?"

"Terrible," he stated, and Zaylie's heart dropped. "I just spoke with Odin; he told me what happened. This is crazy, Zaylie."

Zaylie sighed. "Yes, it is. I wish you were well enough to go back to work. I don't feel comfortable with Odin Carter handling the case."

"He's more familiar with it, though, than I am," Bill replied. "He's the one who headed up this investigation over fifty years ago, you know."

"Which is why we don't want him handling it again this time," Gran spoke up. "He was against Azalea back then, and he still is now."

"I'm sorry, Mrs. Ferguson," Bill said. "I wish there was more that I could do. Look, Zaylie, will you head down to the station to give a DNA sample? Since you're the only blood relative on the island at the moment, that's going to be the best way to identify the body. Odin hasn't done this in a long time, so I told him I'd help as much as I can from home."

Nodding, Zaylie closed the diary and jumped to her feet. "Sure," she replied. "I'll be there in a few minutes."

Thirty minutes later, the DNA sample was finished and Zaylie was already leaving the station. As she headed out, she saw Sheriff Carter standing at the front desk, talking to one of the officers.

"Do you have any idea how long it will take to get the sample processed?" she asked him, failing to notice the man who had just entered the station.

Sheriff Carter shook his head. "I don't know, Miss Layne," he told her, his tone slightly peeved. "Back in my day, it would have taken a good two weeks. Nowadays, you young people want everything rushed."

"We're just anxious to know the results," Zaylie replied, trying to be patient. "If you'd found a dead body in your backyard, you'd be curious, too."

"Did you say *dead body*?"

Zaylie and Sheriff Carter turned to find a man in his early forties staring at them with wide eyes.

"Calm down, Rochelle," the sheriff said. "It's at least fifty years old."

Pulling a pen and notepad from his back pocket as swiftly as a gunfighter in the Wild West would draw his pistol, Mr. Rochelle asked, "Could you give me more details?"

It dawned on Zaylie who the man was, and she could have kicked herself for spilling the beans in front of him. "When we find out more, Mr. Rochelle, we'll let the newspaper know," she told him.

With a frown, Mr. Rochelle studied Zaylie for a moment before his eyes flew open wide and he exclaimed, "You're that Layne girl! If you found a fifty-something-year-old body in your yard, then it must belong to the infamous Azalea Layne."

Placing a hand on her hip, Zaylie raised an eyebrow and asked, "Infamous?"

Ignoring her, Rochelle rushed over to Odin's side and said, "Come on, Sheriff. Can't you give me a little hint?"

His lips twitching, Sheriff Carter said, "I really shouldn't, but...well, we're fairly certain it's Azalea Layne."

Zaylie clenched her jaw with frustration. The sheriff had no right to spread any rumors until they were certain, but he'd done it on purpose; she could tell by the smirk on his face.

Mr. Rochelle all but jumped up and down with excitement. He quickly scribbled down some notes on his paper and rushed back out the front door.

"I'll let you know when we get those results back," Sheriff Carter said to Zaylie before shuffling off toward his office.

Zaylie watched him go, wishing she could give

the old man a piece of her mind. With a huff, she spun on her heel and marched out to her car. If her assumptions were correct, the discovery of the supposed "infamous" Azalea Layne's body would be all over the front page tomorrow. People would be flocking to their house and ringing Gran's phone off the hook to ask a million nosy questions.

When Zaylie drove through the gate at Azalea Bluff fifteen minutes later, she couldn't help but smile. She was so happy to be back home; her family had owned the property for generations, and she loved this place. As she gazed out through the windshield at the massive oak trees that lined the driveway and formed a natural arch overhead, she let out a long breath and allowed herself to relax.

When Zaylie rounded the bend and neared the house, she was surprised to see a large van parked out front. "Garner's Plumbing" was painted across the side, and when Zaylie parked her car, she quickly jumped out and hurried inside.

"Gran?" she called out as she walked into the house.

"We're in the living room," Gran responded.

When Zaylie stepped into the living room, her eyes widened when she spotted water dripping from the ceiling.

"We're having plumbing issues again, Zaylie," Gran said with a sigh. "Apparently, that leak in your bathroom a few months ago was never truly fixed." Motioning to a man in his early seventies and another man who was closer to Zaylie's age, she added, "Zaylie, you remember Toby Garner and his grandson, Chase, don't you?"

Toby Garner was one of Gran's oldest friends; Zaylie even suspected they'd been sweethearts during their younger years. She'd heard that his wife had passed away a few months ago and wondered how he'd been coping. Chase, on the other hand, was more of a mystery to Zaylie. He'd always been very quiet and kept to himself. He was somewhat handsome, with thinning blonde hair and blue eyes, but she hadn't seen much of him since they were kids. He'd moved away for several years and had only just moved back to the island.

"Sure, Chase and I used to fight over the old tree house at church," Zaylie replied with a smile. "Hi, Mr. Toby. How are you?"

"Wondering why your grandmother didn't get us to do the job in the first place," he stated, raising an eyebrow at Gran.

Blushing, Gran said, "Now, Toby, I left all of that up to Ryker Steele. He was doing some work on the house during that time, and I just let him handle it."

"That's what happens when you leave things up to these young whippersnappers," Toby grumbled.

"Or just when you leave things up to Ryker Steele," Zaylie muttered under her breath.

Ryker was Rita's twin brother and had always been somewhat of a thorn in Zaylie's side. The two had sort of become friends over the last few months…sort of…but the arrogant man never failed to get her dander up. She'd heard he was dating some girl he'd met in Savannah and Zaylie had barely seen him in weeks, a fact that she wasn't complaining about.

"Well, I'm placing it in your capable hands now," Gran stated as she patted Toby's arm and smiled. "I know it will be fixed right this time."

"Chase, let's head upstairs and figure out what's going on," Toby said, and the two men left the room.

"I declare, if it's not one thing, it's something else," Gran huffed, shaking her head. Grabbing Zaylie's arm, she said in a low tone, "Let's go read some more of the diary."

"Shouldn't we wait until they leave?" Zaylie asked as Gran dragged her through the house and into the kitchen.

"Who knows how long they'll take?" Gran waved a hand. "I'm dying to read more; just read quietly."

Sitting at the table, Zaylie opened the diary and scanned over the first few sentences. "Where was I?" she muttered. "Ah, yes, here we are…"

I've been accused of robbing my father's bank and killing my fiancé…my dearest Russell, how can you be dead? We had so many plans. How could this have happened?

It all started earlier today when I received a note from Russell…

CHAPTER 4

Azalea – 1966

The house was dark and still as I tiptoed down the stairs, clutching a small suitcase in one hand and the note from Russell in the other. He'd secretly passed the note to me at the bank earlier that day. It simply read, *"Tonight is the night,"* but I knew what it meant. We were going to elope. We'd been discussing it for days, and now that the time was here, I was both excited and terrified.

I stopped at the bottom of the staircase and gazed at my parent's bedroom for a moment. Papa would be furious; he didn't approve of Russell and didn't want us to marry. Russell was eight years older than me and had already served his time in the military, but Papa thought I should marry the son of one of his business partners. Although I was eighteen and could live my life as I chose, I still wished for my parents' approval.

Squaring my shoulders, I continued through the silent house toward the kitchen. The back door squeaked loudly when I pushed it open and I paused, my heart pounding. Had they heard me? When no other sound echoed in the house except for the old grandfather clock, I stepped outside and eased the door shut.

I hurried across the backyard toward the carriage house, hoping they wouldn't hear me when I cranked my car. After shoving the massive door open, I jumped into my car and turned the ignition. The car roared to life, and throwing all caution to the wind, I raced away from the house and my childhood home.

As I bumped along the driveway toward the street, I glanced in the rearview mirror. The house remained dark, and as I rounded the corner, I silently said goodbye. My headlights reflected off the iron gate that led to our property, and as I stopped my car and jumped out, I noticed how cool the breeze felt. It whispered softly through the trees, and as I swung the gate open, I realized how tense I was. Suddenly, a hissing sound came from my right, and with a gasp, I spun around.

There, in the darkness, two golden eyes glittered back at me. *A raccoon,* I thought with a sigh. Shaking myself, I hurried back to my car and drove away, not bothering to close the gate behind me.

It took fifteen minutes to reach the downtown area, and I parked my car in an empty lot just down from the bank. I climbed out and grabbed my suitcase, hoping Papa would find the car before some vagrant stole it. I hated doing this to my parents, but I loved Russell and didn't want to live without him. If only they would try to understand...

I could hear the church bells ringing in the distance; it was two o'clock in the morning. I needed to hurry. Shutting the car door, I rushed down the dark streets, fighting off a sudden sense of foreboding. I was almost at the bank; I could see its lights twinkling through the darkness up ahead. My legs were trembling with exhilaration, and I pushed myself to go faster.

Suddenly, the sound of gunfire split the night air. I stumbled to a halt, my heart catching as I glanced wildly about. Where had the sound come from? Just then, I heard the sound of a door opening, and I looked ahead to see a dark figure running from the bank. With wide eyes, I raised a hand to my chest, the note from Russell floating from my grasp as I ran toward the bank.

"Russell?" I cried out as I hurried through the front door. Squinting in the dim lighting, I could see that the back room door was ajar and the safe appeared to be standing open.

Suddenly, a moan sounded from the back room, and I rushed forward to find Russell lying on the floor with a bullet in his chest.

"Oh, darling," I gasped as I kneeled at his side. "What happened?"

"S-someone robbed th-the safe," he whispered, his hand clutching mine. His eyes were wide with fear, and I felt warm tears dripping down my cheeks.

When I tried to pull my hand away, he gripped it even harder, and I said, "I need to call the police and get you to the hospital."

"No." He shook his head. "Stay...stay w-with me."

The life was fading from his body; I could see it on his face. "I can't," I whispered tearfully. "I've got to get some help."

I stood to my feet and rushed over to the phone. Just as I picked up the receiver, I heard sirens in the distance. Glancing over at Russell, my heart felt as if it had stopped. It was too late to call for help; he was already dead.

When the police arrived, they found me standing over Russell's body with a glazed-over expression on my face.

"Miss Layne?" one of the officers asked as he reached out to touch my arm hesitantly. "Is that you, Miss Layne?"

"He's dead," I mumbled, barely able to comprehend what was happening. Turning, I looked at the young officer through blurry eyes and said, "My fiancé...he's dead."

"What happened?" he asked, glancing between me and the body. "Did...did you have a lover's quarrel? What did you do with the gun?"

My forehead wrinkled in confusion at his question. "I-I don't understand," I replied softly, shaking my head.

More officers entered the room then, and I was escorted from the building. The next hour passed in a blur. I was driven to the police station, where Mama and Papa came to meet me. They were nearly hysterical with worry, and when they saw me, they raced to my side and enveloped me in a tight embrace.

"Thank God you're all right," Papa said in a raspy voice. Pulling back to look at me, he asked, "What were you thinking, girl, running off like that?"

"Russell and I were going to elope," I told him, tears streaming down my cheeks. "But s-someone shot him."

"What?" Mama gasped. "Russell has been shot?"

"The bank was also robbed," a voice sounded from behind, and we all turned to look at Sheriff Odin Carter. He was a young man, barely twenty-five, and Papa didn't think he ought to be sheriff. Odin's father had been the sheriff of Whisper Island for nearly fifty years, though, and he'd seen to it that his son took over once he retired.

"The bank was robbed?" Papa asked, his face losing all its color. "Oh, good heavens. I need to let my partners know…"

"Russell is also dead," Odin stated. "So, we're not just dealing with a robbery. We're also dealing with murder."

Mama sank into a nearby chair, her tiny hands trembling over the news. I stood beside her like a wooden statue, my heart twisting painfully within my chest.

"Miss Layne, if you would follow me, I'd like to ask you a few questions."

Nodding, I quietly moved forward to follow Odin. When Papa came behind me, Odin held out his hand and said, "Alone. I'll need to question her alone."

Papa frowned. "Question her? Carter, what is going on?" he demanded.

His jaw clenching over the authoritative tone in Papa's voice, Odin stated, "She was found at a crime scene, Mr. Layne, standing over the body. I'm only following procedure by questioning her."

"So…so I'm a suspect?" I gasped, my eyes widening.

Stepping aside, Odin motioned down the hall to his left and said, "Please, walk this way. *Now*."

"We'll be right out here, honey," Papa called as I walked down the hall and into a cold room with a table and two chairs.

I sat in one of the chairs and wrapped my arms around my trembling body. Odin sat across from me, his piercing blue eyes seeming to stare a hole right through me.

"Miss Layne, please tell me exactly what happened tonight," he said, his voice echoing off the bare walls.

As I recounted the story, Odin took notes. When I came to the part of finding Russell lying on the floor in a puddle of blood, I broke down and began to cry once again. As I cried, the room was still and silent. I could feel Odin watching me, and I told myself to get it together. Now was not the time to break down; Russell's killer needed to be brought to justice.

"Miss Layne," Odin spoke out, breaking the silence, "you can stop with the fake tears. I know you were somehow involved in this."

Dropping my hands from my face, I stared at Odin as if he'd lost his mind. "*What?*" I gasped.

His lips were held in a firm line, but one eyebrow was cocked in a very condescending way. "Look, Azalea, we've known each other for years," he stated. "You may be younger than me, but I've always...well, noticed you. You're miserable with your life; I've known that for years. You might fool everyone else around you, but you can't fool me."

As he spoke, I slowly sat back in my chair and watched him, my tears dry as my green gaze pierced through his like a cat's.

"Why don't you just tell me the truth?" he asked. "If you do, I might be able to help you. So tell me... who is your partner? Did he promise that the two of you would run away with the diamonds if you helped him tonight? Look, just tell me where you hid the gun, and I'll be sure to put in a good word for you with the DA."

With a clenched jaw, I slowly stood to my feet and said in a steely tone, "I don't have to listen to this. If you wish to question me further, you'll do it with my lawyer present."

As I stalked from the room, Odin watched me go with a knowing look on his face.

CHAPTER 5

Zaylie

The sound of footsteps as they neared the kitchen interrupted Zaylie as she read, and she quickly closed the diary and set it down.

"Louella?" a voice called out.

"We're in the kitchen, Toby," Gran replied.

The kitchen door swung open, and both men stepped inside. Mr. Garner wore a frown on his weathered face, while Chase glanced curiously at the old book resting on the table.

"Are we interrupting?" he asked, still studying the book.

Quickly slipping the diary beneath her hands, Zaylie shook her head and said, "No, certainly not."

"That wall upstairs is going to have to be opened up," Toby announced, jumping right into it. "We can do it, but you'll need to get Ryker back out to fix it once we're finished."

"Oh, dear," Gran sighed. "It's that bad?"

Toby shrugged. "It would seem so, but we won't know how bad until we get that wall open."

Zaylie groaned. "I guess I'll need to move my things out of the bathroom again," she said.

"That would probably be for the best," Toby agreed. "Unless you don't mind drywall dust being all over your bathroom towels."

"I'll move everything out," Zaylie replied with a small chuckle.

"We've got to pick up a few supplies at the hardware store, and then we can come back and start today," Toby said. "Will that be okay with the two of you?"

Zaylie and Gran looked at each other, and then in unison, they said, "That's fine with us."

While the two men headed to the store, Zaylie ran upstairs and transferred everything from her bathroom to the guest bathroom. She'd just finished when Toby and Chase got back.

When Zaylie stepped into the kitchen, Gran nodded toward the diary that still rested on the table and said in a low voice, "I think we should keep that somewhere safe while the men are working in the house; I didn't like the way that boy was looking at it."

Zaylie couldn't help but laugh. "Gran, "that boy" just happens to be the same age as me," she stated.

"Honey, when you're my age, anyone under fifty is considered young," Gran retorted.

Shaking her head, Zaylie put the diary into one of the kitchen drawers and said, "I think I'm going to pay old Mr. Whitlock a visit."

Gran raised her eyebrows in surprise. "This late in the day? I don't know if he'll see you," she replied. "Like I said earlier, he's been a recluse for years."

Zaylie shrugged. "It's worth a shot, though," she said. "I think I'll take Smutti with me; maybe he likes dogs."

Twenty minutes later, Zaylie turned her car down a long and winding dirt road. The trees and shrubbery were terribly overgrown, and Zaylie stopped her car for a moment to double-check the address on her phone.

This looks right, she thought, glancing warily around. *No wonder he's a recluse; not many people would want to drive in here.*

Putting her foot back on the gas, Zaylie proceeded forward, hoping the old man didn't fancy taking shots at strangers who entered his property unannounced. Perhaps Gran had been right and Zaylie shouldn't have decided to pay a visit so late in the day.

As she rounded the corner, a shabby, one-story house came into view. A few of the windows were broken, the shutters hung loosely on their hinges, and weeds grew so high around the front porch that Zaylie wasn't certain she could walk up the steps without getting scratched. She put the car in park and stared at the old place, wondering if this was such a good idea.

After a moment of deliberation, Zaylie took a deep breath and climbed out of the car. Something told her Mr. Whitlock probably didn't care for pets, so she left Smutti in the car with the engine still running.

"Who knows, I may need to make a quick exit," she said to the dog before shutting the car door.

Zaylie cautiously walked across the yard and climbed gingerly up the rickety porch steps, doing all she could to avoid the thorns and vines that reached out for her shins. Once she reached the front door, she knocked twice and called out, announcing herself.

"I'm Azalea Layne's great-niece," she said loudly. "I was hoping you could talk to me for a few minutes."

She could hear a shuffling coming from inside the house, and after a moment, the door slowly creaked open. A man who looked to be in his upper 80s peered out at her with suspicious eyes. It was obvious he used to be a very large man, but he was now thin and frail, with stooped-over shoulders and a scraggly white beard.

"What do you want?" he asked in a gruff voice.

"I'm sorry to bother you, Mr. Whitlock," Zaylie said hesitantly, "but I was wondering if you could answer a couple of questions about my great-aunt Azalea Layne?"

Bushy eyebrows lowered over faded brown eyes as the old man frowned at her. "I-I don't like talking to strangers," he stated and began to close the door.

"But we believe we just found her body in our backyard," Zaylie hurriedly stated.

Mr. Whitlock paused, and then the door swung back open. "Somebody killed her?" he wanted to know.

Zaylie's head tilted to one side. "Yes, but how did you know that?" she asked curiously.

"I always knew somebody'd do it, sooner or later," he replied. "She was achin' for a breakin', that woman."

"What do you mean?" Zaylie wanted to know.

"When I was working at the house, I heard stuff," he replied, shrugging.

"Stuff that people around town were saying?" Zaylie asked.

Mr. Whitlock shook his head. "Nope," he stated. "Stuff that *she* was saying."

Zaylie's brow furrowed. "Like what?" she pressed.

Opening his mouth, Mr. Whitlock hesitated and stared at Zaylie for a moment. Something changed in his expression, and with narrowed eyes, he said in a steely tone, "Never mind. Like I said, girl, I don't like talking to strangers. Now git."

Not willing to give in just yet, Zaylie put her hand firmly on the door to keep him from closing it again. "Mr. Whitlock, *please.* Couldn't you just answer a few more questions?"

Bringing two bony fingers up to his lips, Mr. Whitlock let out a sharp, shrill whistle, and Zaylie stepped back in surprise. When she looked at him questioningly, he sneered and said, "Don't say I didn't warn ya."

As soon as he slammed the door in her face, she heard it; the sound of pounding footsteps as someone...or *something*...raced through the trees toward the house. Spinning around, Zaylie squinted and searched the property, her heart pounding. Movement out of the corner of her eye caught her attention, and when she looked in that direction, she gasped. A massive Rottweiler was racing directly toward her, its teeth bared and ready for blood.

Shaking herself, Zaylie leaped off the porch and ran toward her car. Smutti barked ferociously from the back seat as she scratched frantically at the window, trying to get out to defend her master. The Rottweiler was only a few feet away, and with adrenaline pumping through her veins, Zaylie dove for the passenger side door. She jerked it open and launched herself inside, barely slamming the door shut just before the dog lunged at the window. Zaylie stared at the massive creature, her chest heaving as she watched its mighty paws claw and pound at her door. Its snarls and growls sent chills down her spine, and she quickly gave Smutti the command to stand down.

After a moment, the dog moved away from the car to stand on the rickety porch steps, its beady eyes never leaving her. Swallowing past the lump in her throat, Zaylie pushed herself across the console and drove from the property. Just before rounding the bend, she glanced in the rearview mirror to find that the dog was following her as if to make certain she really was leaving.

Chase Garner walked down the stairs in the Layne house, his beady eyes taking in the priceless antiques and expensive furnishings throughout the house. The Laynes were obviously very well off, but the thing that had caught his attention the most was that old book the two women had been reading in the kitchen. The way Zaylie had quickly hidden it beneath her hands let him know it was something important.

Plus, he'd heard them reading a little of it when he and his granddad were walking toward the kitchen. Zaylie had said something about someone running off with diamonds. Did the book have something to do with that body they'd found in the backyard? Chase wasn't sure, but he intended to find out. Perhaps his grandfather would know; he seemed to know a lot of things when it came to the Layne family.

CHAPTER 6

Zaylie

On her way back home, Zaylie stopped by the market to grab some last-minute groceries. It was after six o'clock and everyone had apparently decided to go shopping after work. When she spotted Helen Buchanan, she almost turned the other way, but it was too late. The woman had already seen her.

"I didn't know dogs were allowed in here," the woman stated, her lips pursed into a disapproving line.

"The owner, Mr. Davenport, doesn't mind if I bring Smutti in sometimes," Zaylie replied with a forced smile.

Still frowning, Helen cocked an eyebrow and said, "I guess I won't complain then, especially since she's technically a working dog."

"I appreciate that," Zaylie said politely.

As she pushed her buggy past the older woman, it was all she could do not to roll her eyes. What Rita and Ryker's dad saw in that woman, Zaylie would never know. The only logical explanation was the poor man was so lonely after his wife's death that he wasn't thinking clearly.

"I won't complain either," a deep voice spoke up from her left. "I happen to like dogs."

Turning, Zaylie grinned at her ex-boyfriend, Micah Pierce, and said, "Since you're a veterinarian, you'd better like dogs."

Micah laughed as he leaned over to pet Smutti. "I can't figure out why Mr. Steele is dating her," he said in a low voice.

"I get the feeling *she* pursued *him*," Zaylie replied with a snicker. "Let's just hope she doesn't propose or Rita will have a stroke."

Chuckling, Micah stood up straight and said, "We certainly don't want that to happen. So, how have you been lately? I haven't seen much of you in the last couple of months."

With a sigh, Zaylie told him about the discovery of the body in their backyard. "We think it's my great aunt Azalea," she said.

Micah's eyes had widened throughout the story, and with a shake of his head, he asked, "Is it just me, or have a lot of crazy things started happening since you came back to the island?"

Crossing her arms, Zaylie stated in a sassy tone, "Well, it's not *my* fault."

Micah raised an eyebrow and said matter-of-factly, "The body was discovered because of the groundbreaking for your new training center."

Chewing on her bottom lip, Zaylie admitted with a nod, "Yeah, that's true. How crazy is it, though, to think that a body has been buried on our property for years and we never knew?"

"That's a little creepy," Micah agreed. "What did the sheriff say? Is he going to investigate?"

Zaylie shrugged. "Who knows with that man? I wish Uncle Bill was able to handle it."

Glancing at his watch, Micah said, "I've got to go, but I hope you'll keep me updated?" When Zaylie nodded, he hesitated for a brief moment and then added, "Hey, I recently finished refurbishing Dad's old boat, and I was wondering if you would like to go out on the water with me sometime?"

Zaylie blinked in surprise. Was he asking her on a date or simply being nice? She didn't want to make a big deal about it, so she smiled and said she'd love to. As she watched him walk away with his basketful of groceries, she wondered if she'd done the right thing. She hadn't seen much of him in the last two months; she'd been too busy going to and from the training center in Tennessee as she prepared for her move back to the island. Was she ready to so easily drift back into a friendship with the man she'd once loved...the man who cheated on her and broke her heart? That happened so long ago, though. People could change, after all.

By the time Zaylie got back to Azalea Bluff, it was beginning to get dark. Crickets and cicadas sang loudly from the trees and bushes, and a salty breeze ruffled Zaylie's auburn hair as she carried the groceries inside.

She'd just stepped into the kitchen and placed the bag of groceries on the counter when her cell phone started to ring. Pulling her phone from her purse, Zaylie was a bit surprised to find that the caller was her mother, Stephanie.

"Hi, mom," she answered the call.

"Zaylie, maybe you should rethink this new training center venture," her mother immediately said.

Her brow furrowing, Zaylie asked, "Why do you say that?"

"I just spoke with Mama, and she told me what happened today," Stephanie replied. "Maybe moving back to the island wasn't such a good idea."

Zaylie sighed inwardly. Why did Gran have to spill the beans to Stephanie so soon?

"Mom, if the body really does belong to Azalea, don't you think it's a good thing we finally found her so she can be put to rest?" Zaylie asked.

"I just don't like the idea of you getting involved in another murder case," Stephanie stated.

Zaylie knew that wasn't the entire reason. Her mom still struggled with the painful memories related to the island and Azalea Bluff and had been against her daughter's return from the beginning. Zaylie knew she had to be careful, though, with what she said. She and her mother had only recently made amends with each other, and Zaylie didn't wish to drive another wedge between them.

"I'll be careful," Zaylie promised. "I imagine whoever killed her is long gone by now anyway."

Zaylie changed the subject then, but the conversation didn't last very long. Things were still a bit stiff and awkward between them, but Zaylie was grateful they were both attempting to mend their relationship.

After the call was over, Zaylie put away all the groceries and went searching for Gran. She was sitting on the back deck, looking out over the river and marsh as the few remaining streaks of pink and orange from the sunset faded away.

"Did Mr. Toby and Chase get finished?" she asked as she sat next to Gran.

Gran shook her head. "No," she replied. "It's worse than they thought, I'm afraid. They're coming back tomorrow to work some more."

Zaylie groaned. "That's great," she muttered. "I hope it doesn't take forever to get it fixed."

Looking over at her granddaughter, Gran asked, "How did it go with Mr. Whitlock?"

With a sheepish expression, Zaylie said, "It didn't, unfortunately. You were right, Gran. The man hates visitors. He did say one thing that puzzled me, though."

"What's that?" Gran wanted to know.

"He said he knew someone would kill Azalea sooner or later," Zaylie replied. "He said that while he was working on the house, he overheard some things but wouldn't tell me what."

Gran frowned. "How strange," she murmured. After a moment, she stood up and said, "I'm going inside to take a shower, and then I want to read more of Azalea's diary."

Nodding eagerly, Zaylie hurried upstairs to take

a shower of her own in the guest bathroom. She hated not being in her own bathroom and hoped the Garners would be able to get finished soon. As she stepped from the shower ten minutes later, she quickly tied her wet hair up in a towel, slipped into a bathrobe and fuzzy slippers, and hurried back downstairs.

Gran was already in the living room waiting, and after Zaylie fixed herself a glass of sweet tea, she joined her grandmother on the sofa. Opening the diary, Zaylie began to read.

After I marched from the interrogation room, I ran to Papa and begged him to take me home. Odin followed and said that before I could leave, I had to get fingerprinted. This whole thing is so humiliating. I half expected Odin to demand I stay until I could get a lawyer, but I guess he knows he doesn't have enough evidence against me yet.

The drive home was tense and uncomfortable. Mama and Papa are very upset with me. When we got back home, they sat me down and wanted to know what I'd been thinking by planning to elope. Why can't they understand that all I've wanted these last several months is to marry Russell? Neither of them will accept it, though.

I don't understand why they've been so against Russell. He may not be what Papa considers an appropriate suitor, but he's kind and caring and he loves me. Was it so wrong for us to go against my parent's wishes and try to create a life for ourselves?

Now that he's dead, I don't know what I'm going to do. Odin thinks I stole those diamonds and he'll keep on until he finds something, anything, that points to me. I've got to find out who really stole them, and fast...

CHAPTER 7

Azalea - 1966

As I paced around my room, a million thoughts ran through my head. The only thing that made any sense to me was that one of Papa's business partners, or their immediate family, was responsible for the theft and shooting of Russell. The fact that I could even consider such a thing, though, made me sick to my stomach, as Papa's partners were like family to me and my older brother, Joseph.

First, there was Harold Beecher, or "Big Hal" as we all liked to call him since he was such a beast of a man. He was an old childhood friend of Papa's. They went to college together, always dreaming of opening their own bank someday. After their dream came to fruition, Big Hal met and married a rich widow, Mildred. Instead of selling his share of the bank and retiring, however, he wanted to continue working instead of living off of his wife's money. His diamonds were the ones stolen; he'd planned to surprise his wife with them on their upcoming wedding anniversary.

Then there was also James Cook, or "Cookie" as everyone lovingly called him. Papa and Big Hal met him in college, and they all instantly became good friends. Cookie had a head for business and a wonderfully friendly, outgoing personality. Papa always said he was the main one responsible for getting their clients, as no one could resist his charm.

I sat at my window seat and stared out into the night. Who would benefit the most from stealing those diamonds? Big Hal would collect the insurance, but he certainly didn't need the money, as his wife had millions. Unless he wanted to leave her and knew she wouldn't give him anything in a divorce. Big Hal seemed to love Mildred dearly, though. Their son, Dale, was obnoxious and I disliked him a great deal. He was a few years older than me and seemed to think he was better than everyone else. Was he capable of pulling off such a heist, though? He was in the reserves but had opted to be sent back home to study a skill and I hadn't seen much of him in the last few months.

Cookie was so loveable that I couldn't think he was responsible. The same couldn't be said, however, for his wife. "Cynical" Cynthia is what my best friend Louella and I called her. She seemed to always look down her nose at everyone, but would she ever lower herself enough to rob a bank? I doubted it. Their daughter, Brenda, was just as friendly and fun-loving as her father, but she also loved attention. She and a few of her friends always seemed to be getting into trouble together. Could they have robbed the bank as some sort of prank and things somehow went too far?

With a moan, I stood up to continue pacing. How was I ever going to figure out who stole those diamonds? With my parents watching my every move and Odin breathing down my neck, it wasn't going to be easy. I had to try, though, for Russell's sake.

The next morning, I was surprised to find my brother, Joseph, sitting in the kitchen with my parents. Since his marriage last summer, I rarely saw him anymore. He and his wife now lived in Savannah, and even though that wasn't very far away, he seemed to be too busy for us anymore. Papa had always thought Joseph would take over the bank someday. After marrying Annemarie, however, he'd decided to join his father-in-law's law practice, much to everyone's disappointment. Joseph had already undergone four years of undergrad study and had three years left of law school.

"Hey, sis," he said when he saw me.

Joseph and I had always been close, and even though I'd never admit it to anyone, I resented his wife for taking him away from us. We rarely saw him since his marriage to Annemarie, and it always felt a little awkward at first when he would pay us a visit.

"Hi," I replied, giving him a quick hug before pulling away.

Everyone stared at me in silence for a moment. I wasn't sure if it was because I looked like I'd been run over by a team of horses or because of everything that had happened the night before. Giving them all a tight-lipped smile, I set about making myself a cup of coffee.

"Azalea," Joseph began, clearing his throat, "Mom and Pop called me this morning and asked if I could come over. They told me everything that happened, and it sounds like you might need a good lawyer."

"Will your father-in-law's firm represent me, or would that be too much of a scandal?" I asked in a slightly snarky tone.

"Azalea, please don't be difficult," Mama said with a sigh. "Your brother is willing to do whatever he can to help you. Aren't you, Joseph?"

I didn't miss the way Joseph hesitated and averted his eyes, and it was all I could do not to smirk. Ever since he'd married Annemarie, the most important thing in life had become upholding her family's name and reputation. Annemarie's father was very particular about what cases he would allow his firm to take, and I was curious how much influence Joseph had there...or how far he was willing to go for his sister.

"Of course," Joseph finally answered. "I plan to talk to Mr. Yarrow this afternoon when he comes into the office. Azalea, is there anything I should know? You haven't kept anything from us, have you?"

I hesitated, but before I could answer, the doorbell rang. Mother immediately jumped up and hurried from the kitchen to answer the door, and as I grabbed the sugar from the cabinet, I kept one ear trained on the voices I heard. Did one of them belong to Sheriff Odin?

Seconds later, Mother returned, her face pale and hands clutched together in front of her slender waist. Odin and one of his deputies stepped into the kitchen behind her, and by the looks on all their faces, I knew something was wrong.

"Azalea, you're going to have to come with us," Odin spoke up.

Taking a step back, I asked, "Why?"

His eyes glinting with satisfaction, Odin stated, "Your fingerprints were found all over the safe. Azalea Layne, you're under arrest for robbery and suspicion of murder."

CHAPTER 8

Zaylie

With a shake of her head, Zaylie closed the diary and said, "This story just keeps getting more and more crazy." Glancing over at her grandmother, she asked, "Gran, do you think Granddad Joseph believed his sister was guilty? He never talked about her, you know."

"No, I think talking about the whole situation was just too painful for him," Gran replied. "In a way, I think he blamed himself for her disappearance."

"Why?"

"He felt like he should have been here instead of in Savannah," she said as she took a sip of hot tea. "After Azalea disappeared, he put his foot down and left his father-in-law's practice to come back here. He and your grandmother moved into the house; his mother came back to live with them until she died."

"Was Gramma Annemarie not happy here?" Zaylie asked.

"Not at first," Gran replied. "But once Joseph established his own law practice and they had your father, she came to love this place as much as the rest of us." Leaning over to pat Zaylie's hand, she added with a small smile, "Even though Joseph rarely mentioned Azalea, he wanted your dad to name one of you girls after her. Your mom was stuck on the name Zoe for your sister, but when you were born, your dad decided on Zaylie, which is a shortened form of Azalea. Joseph was very happy about that, and you do look so much like her."

Zaylie smiled. "It's too bad I wasn't able to meet her," she said.

The two said good night then and went their separate ways to prepare for bed. As Zaylie settled down and tried to read a book, she realized her head was starting to ache. Apparently, trying to read the old, faded handwriting in the diary was causing a bit of eye strain. She was just about to go downstairs to look for some Tylenol when her phone chimed, alerting her to a malfunction in the app that automatically opened and closed the gate to their property. Zaylie restarted her phone and then tried to reset the app, but nothing was working. With a sigh, she resolved to just go close the gate herself.

Not wishing to bother Gran with the noisy garage door, Zaylie decided to walk. It was nearly a mile to the gate, but she thought the fresh air and exercise would do her some good. Deciding to leave Smutti asleep in her bed, Zaylie changed into her tennis shoes and sneaked out.

The night was balmy but cool, and the sky was clear. As Zaylie headed down the long, dark driveway, she noticed how unusually quiet it was. The owls and night birds were silent, and even the crickets and cicadas weren't singing. *How odd,* Zaylie thought.

The light from the moon drifted between the tree branches overhead, casting unearthly shadows all around. Feeling a little uneasy, Zaylie clicked on her flashlight and quickened her steps, her eyes darting cautiously about. Silky strands of Spanish moss drifted lifelessly back and forth in the gentle breeze, and Zaylie wondered why the familiar surroundings suddenly seemed so ominous. Was it the fact that a dead body had been found on the property, or was it something else?

Zaylie breathed a sigh of relief when she finally reached the gate. Tucking the flashlight into her back pocket, she grasped the old iron railings, but before she could swing the gate shut, the sound of a snapping twig caught her attention. Turning, Zaylie shined the flashlight into the woods beside her. Shadows danced all around and the bushes stirred a bit in the breeze, but she couldn't see anything else. Perhaps it was just an animal. Shrugging it off, Zaylie returned to the task at hand and swung the gate shut.

Just then, she heard a rustling in the bushes only a few feet away. With a gasp, Zaylie jerked around, her eyes wide as she once again searched the thick foliage. She couldn't see a thing, but something told her that someone...or something...was out there, watching her.

Her brain began sending off warning signals, and with trembling fingers, Zaylie quickly locked the gate and took off back down the driveway. As she walked, she kept looking around, waiting for someone to jump out at her. *Oh, why didn't I bring my phone?* She thought, her heart pounding. She then stopped and took a deep breath. Why was she overreacting so? Most likely, the only thing she'd heard was a deer or a raccoon. Why was she letting her imagination run away so?

Suddenly, another twig snapped, and then another, followed by the undeniable sound of footsteps on the forest floor. And they were getting closer.

Breaking into a run, Zaylie raced down the driveway like an athlete at breakneck speed. She clutched the flashlight in one hand, ready to use it as a weapon if necessary. Were the footsteps still following? She couldn't be sure; all she could hear was the pounding of her own feet and her short, quick breaths. She often jogged for exercise, but running a mile flat out wasn't something she was used to, and her heart was racing. She pushed herself to go faster, though. An urgency to get inside where it was safe coursed through her veins like a rushing river.

She rounded the corner and could see the house up ahead in the moonlight. Her lungs were screaming for air, but she wouldn't stop. All she could see in her mind's eye was Great Aunt Azalea, as she fought for her own life over fifty years ago. Had she tried to run, too, but was stopped by a bullet in the back? Zaylie wouldn't end up like her; she wouldn't.

She finally reached the house, and without slowing down, she leaped up the steps and onto the front porch. She stopped at the front door, her chest heaving, and slowly turned around. Her entire body trembled as she searched the darkness. She saw nothing and suddenly felt very foolish. Why would anyone want to harm her? There was no one sneaking around the property; she'd once again let her imagination get the better of her.

Walking quietly into the house, Zaylie closed the front door and locked it, just in case. As she headed upstairs to bed, she once again thought of Azalea and wondered if this place would ever truly be free of its ghosts.

CHAPTER 9

Zaylie

The next morning when Zaylie entered the kitchen, she noticed that Gran wore a tight expression, and she immediately asked what was wrong.

"Just look at this," Gran said, thrusting the morning newspaper at Zaylie.

"THE BODY OF INFAMOUS JEWEL THIEF, AZALEA LAYNE, HAS FINALLY BEEN FOUND."

Zaylie stared at the headline, her jaw clenching in anger. It had not yet been confirmed that the body belonged to Azalea, and the paper had no right to accuse her of stealing those diamonds when there was no real proof.

"Should we sue?" Zaylie asked in disgust.

Her lips pursed, Gran shook her head and said, "That's exactly what I feel like doing. How dare they print such nonsense?"

Zaylie opened the refrigerator and pulled out a carton of eggs. "Now everyone in town will be talking about it and asking all sorts of nosy questions," she said as she cracked two eggs into a bowl.

Gran sighed. "It feels like 1966 all over again,"

she said, and Zaylie thought she heard tears in her voice.

"I'm sorry, Gran," Zaylie said. "Do you think…"

Before she could finish, the doorbell rang and Gran hurried through the house to open the front door. As Zaylie poured her eggs into the skillet, she could hear Mr. Garner and Chase talking in the foyer. When Gran asked if they'd like some coffee, Zaylie was glad she'd remembered to get dressed this morning.

"Don't mind if I do," Mr. Toby said, and seconds later, they all three entered the kitchen.

Zaylie greeted the two men, and while Gran poured the coffee, she noticed Chase eyeing the newspaper lying on the table. After a moment, he said, "Granddad was telling me about that article on the front page this morning. Do you really think the body is Azalea Layne's?"

Zaylie thought his question was a bit tactless, but she didn't say anything. Instead, she quietly continued scrambling her eggs while Gran answered.

"We don't know yet," Gran replied. With a tight smile, she handed the coffee to the men and asked, "Would you like cream and sugar?"

Mr. Toby shook his head while Chase said, "Sugar, please." While Gran grabbed the sugar bowl, he added, "Granddad said it was never proven that Azalea stole those diamonds."

Mr. Toby cleared his throat and gave his grandson a look. "That was a long time ago," he stated. "I think it was ridiculous for the newspaper to have printed all that heresy."

Taking the sugar bowl back from Chase and setting it down on the counter with a loud *plunk*, Gran nodded indignantly and said, "I couldn't agree with you more, Toby." Looking at Chase, she added tartly, "And no, young man, it was never proven to be true."

An awkward silence filled the room then, and after taking a few gulps of their coffee, both men said it was time they got to work. They'd barely left the kitchen when the back door flew open and Rita breezed in carrying a large, unidentifiable object.

"Y'all, this is so exciting," she cried, shoving her sunglasses on top of her head.

Raising her eyebrows, Zaylie asked, "What is?"

Rita looked at her friend like she was crazy. "The whole story behind your great aunt, silly! Look, I brought along this metal detector; I thought we should start searching the yard immediately."

With pursed lips, Gran marched over to Zaylie's best friend and asked, "And what exactly do you expect to find? Azalea did *not* steal those diamonds."

Rita frowned at Gran. "Someone killed her, though, didn't they?" she asked matter-of-factly. "Why would anyone have killed her if she didn't have the diamonds?"

"I don't know," Gran cried, throwing her hands in the air. "Maybe because she was trying to uncover a thief and murderer and stumbled upon more than she could handle."

It was obvious by her expression that Rita wasn't ready to let it go, and before her best friend and grandmother could get into an all-out war, Zaylie quickly intervened. "Rita, I don't know that a metal detector could find diamonds anyway," she stated.

Rita glanced down at the contraption and sighed. "You're probably right," she muttered, eyeing Gran as the older woman sat down with a huff.

Honestly, these two are as bad as each other, Zaylie thought.

"Why don't we leave it up to the police?" she asked with a small smile.

Rita raised one eyebrow and gave her friend a look. "Oh, is that what you were doing yesterday when you almost got eaten by that Rottweiler?" she asked drolly.

"Fine, you've made your point," Zaylie replied, shaking her head as she placed a slice of bread in the toaster. "Apparently, this family is too nosy for its own good."

Gran's phone rang just then, and when she saw who it was, she groaned. "Speaking of nosy," she muttered as she answered the call. "Hi, Sophia. Yes, I saw it. No, I didn't know it was going to be in the paper."

The rest of the day was spent dealing with one phone call after another. It seemed the whole town was in an uproar, and Zaylie wondered how long it would take for treasure hunters to start showing up. If that is, Rita didn't find it first.

At two o'clock that afternoon, Sheriff Odin stopped by the house. He wore a rather smug expression on his leathered face as he said, "It's been confirmed; the body belongs to Azalea Layne."

Gran started crying, and Zaylie noticed Mr. Toby and Chase standing at the top of the stairs, listening.

"What now?" Zaylie wanted to know, as she wrapped a supportive arm around Gran's shoulders.

"I'm going to request that a forensics team from Savannah be sent out here to search the area thoroughly," he replied. "I want to make sure we didn't miss anything before I give you the green light to proceed with the groundbreaking."

"How long will that take?" Zaylie wanted to know.

Odin shrugged nonchalantly. "Who knows? Could be weeks."

As he shuffled back to his car, Zaylie watched him with narrowed eyes. Was it just her, or was he deliberately trying to sabotage her plans for the training center? To say the man was annoying was an understatement.

"I'm sorry, honey," Gran sniffled as they made their way into the living room. "This is ruining everything for you."

Tilting her head to one side, Zaylie thought

something over for a moment before saying, "You know, I could always change locations. Sheriff Odin couldn't interfere then, could he?"

Gran's eyes brightened at the idea. "No, I wouldn't think so," she said. "Where else could you put it?"

"How about in that clearing where the old playhouse used to be? I don't know why I didn't think of that place before; it's further back and would probably be better in the long run."

Gran nodded. "That would be perfect," she agreed.

Feeling excited, Zaylie called Uncle Bill, just to make certain her idea would work. When he said it would be fine as long as the construction crew stayed away from the crime scene, she immediately called Alan Whitlock.

"My crew can be out there tomorrow," Alan told her. Clearing his throat, he added, "Uh, my dad told me about your visit. I'm sorry about how he acted, Miss Layne."

Zaylie's cheeks flushed. "No worries, Mr. Whitlock," she quickly said. "I shouldn't have shown up like I did and asked so many questions."

Alan hesitated. "What exactly did you ask him?" he wanted to know. "Dad just said you were asking about Azalea."

"Your dad did some work around the house right before Azalea died," Zaylie explained. "I thought he may have unknowingly witnessed something."

"I'll talk to him about it and see what I can find

out," Alan promised.

Later that afternoon, Mr. Toby and Chase finished up with the plumbing job and told the two women they would need to get Ryker out to fix the wall.

"I'll call him first thing in the morning," Gran said with a wide smile. She'd taken a liking to Ryker Steele, and Zaylie suspected she wished her granddaughter liked him, too.

As Zaylie walked the two men out, Chase asked, "So, there's going to be a forensics team out here poking around?"

Zaylie nodded. "I doubt they'll find anything, though," she replied. "We don't believe that Azalea really stole those diamonds."

Chase looked down at her, his blue eyes piercing as he said, "Well, maybe they'll find a clue as to who murdered her."

A chill swept over Zaylie at the word "murder", and she lightly ran her hands over her arms. "Yes, maybe so," she murmured.

"If not, maybe y'all will find something in that old book you were reading yesterday."

Blinking, Zaylie looked up at Chase to find that he was studying her closely. Before she could respond, Mr. Toby called out to him and he turned to leave. As Zaylie watched them drive away, she wondered how he'd known the book had anything to do with Azalea.

That night, Zaylie and Smutti went into the living room to wait for Gran to get out of the shower so they could read more of the diary. As she waited, Zaylie walked over to Azalea's portrait that had hung on the wall for as long as she could remember. The beautiful emerald eyes glistened mysteriously as they gazed back at Zaylie. Her flaming red hair was cut and styled in the typical 1960s fashion, and she wore a bright green dress that matched her eyes. She was undeniably beautiful, but as Zaylie studied the picture, she wondered for the first time if Great Aunt Azalea had been hiding something all those years ago.

Just then, Smutti stood up and headed toward the kitchen. Hearing the tapping of her claws against the hardwood floor pulled Zaylie's attention away from the picture, and she realized Smutti must need to go outside. She hurried after the dog, who was pacing and whining at the back door, and quickly let her out.

As Smutti sniffed around the yard, Zaylie grabbed a flashlight and walked toward the taped-off area where Azalea's body was found. She stood there, shining the light over the excavated earth, and a chill swept up her spine. This was the final resting place of the beautiful, vibrant young woman from the portrait. What had happened here? Would they find out from Azalea's diary? Zaylie was tempted to skip over to the last few pages, but she knew the whole story wouldn't be in just a few paragraphs. She had a feeling there was a lot written between the lines of that diary that she and Gran would have to interpret.

Suddenly, Smutti raised her nose into the air and her ears immediately went back. Her body stiffened as she faced the tree line behind the house, and a low growl began to rumble past her throat. Zaylie moved to stand beside the dog as she shined the flashlight toward the trees, her thoughts immediately going back to the incident the night before. She couldn't see anything through the dark shadows, but apparently Smutti sensed something. Was it simply a raccoon, or had someone slipped unknowingly onto the property?

Grabbing the dog by the collar, Zaylie said in a firm tone, "Smutti, come," and the two quickly headed back toward the house. They'd just reached the bottom step to the back deck when the sound of a snapping branch split through the night. Smutti spun around and began to bark ferociously, and Zaylie felt her heart jump in her chest.

"Smutti, come inside *now*," she commanded.

The dog reluctantly obeyed and followed her master as Zaylie raced up the steps and into the house. She firmly locked the door behind them and armed the security system.

"Zaylie, I'm ready to read now," Gran called from the living room. "Are you coming?"

"Be there in a second," Zaylie responded.

Just before going to join Gran, Zaylie flipped on the floodlights and peered out the back window. In one split second, she thought she saw a dark silhouette running away from the excavation site, but then it was gone and she told herself that her

imagination was once again getting the better of
her.

CHAPTER 10

Azalea - 1966

Sheriff Odin Carter stood on the other side of the jail cell, staring at me through the bars. He wore a smirk on his face, and I rubbed my arms as a chill swept over me.

"You could always just confess," he stated. "It'll make things easier for all of us."

"I didn't rob the bank, and I didn't shoot Russell," I ground out. "How many times do I have to tell you?"

"Then why were your fingerprints found on the safe?" he asked for the third time that night.

Papa had advised me to wait until I had a lawyer present before I answered any questions, but I just couldn't stand it any longer. Spinning around to face my accuser, I said, "Because I just started working at the bank."

Odin raised his eyebrows. "And part of your new job is manning the safe?" he asked snidely.

"Well, not necessarily," I replied hesitantly. "I had to put a box of some important papers in there for Papa."

His eyes glinting, he stated matter-of-factly, "So, you know the combination to the safe."

Oh, why didn't I keep my big mouth shut? I moaned inwardly.

"I'm not saying another word until my lawyer arrives," I replied tartly.

"If you can find anyone who will represent you," he retorted before stalking away.

I stood all alone in that cold, tiny jail cell and felt the walls closing in on me. What if Odin was right and Joseph couldn't get his father-in-law to agree to represent me? Would Mr. Spell, the one lawyer we had on Whisper Island, help me? I doubted it. Papa was well-respected in the community, but when it came to murder and scandal, people tended to turn their backs on their friends really fast.

Hours passed, and then it was morning. I hadn't slept a wink. My stomach rumbled from hunger, but I wasn't sure I could eat if I tried. What if I was convicted of Russell's murder? I couldn't go to prison; I just couldn't. Being kept behind bars for one night was almost more than I could bear.

At a little past nine o'clock, the sound of approaching footsteps could be heard. I pressed my face against the bars and looked out, relieved to see Joseph and another man walking my way, with Odin in the lead.

"Sis, are you okay?" my brother asked, his face filled with concern.

Forcing myself not to burst into tears, I nodded and said, "Yes, I'm fine."

With a look of disgust on his face, Odin opened

the cell door and said, "You're free to go." When my eyes widened, he pointed a finger in my face and said, "But don't get any ideas about leaving town."

As he stalked away, I looked at Joseph with questioning eyes. Motioning toward the young man at his side, Joseph said, "Azalea, this is Lloyd Johnson. He's with my father-in-law's firm and will be representing you."

Shaking Lloyd's hand, I was struck by how young he looked. He couldn't be more than thirty, and I wondered how much experience he had. As long as there was someone willing to help me, though, I wouldn't complain.

"How did you talk Odin into releasing me?" I asked as the three of us left the station.

"I was able to get you out on bail," Lloyd replied. "You're still not out of the woods yet, but at least you can be at home where you're more comfortable."

I smiled at my brother and Lloyd. "Thank you both so much," I told them.

As we headed toward my brother's car, I breathed in the cool morning air and sighed. It felt so good to be out in the open again; to feel free. As we drove home, I glanced back at the police station and swore to myself to do whatever it took to never return there again.

The next day, Mama mentioned something about Brenda Cook's twentieth birthday party.

Cynthia and Cookie had invited us weeks ago, but Mama wasn't sure we should go.

"I don't think we should hide ourselves away," Papa stated. "It makes us look like we're guilty or ashamed."

Glancing uncertainly at me, Mama said softly, "I don't know if Azalea is up to it, though."

"On the contrary, Mama, I think it would do me good," I said.

What neither of my parents suspected was that I was on a mission to find out who stole those diamonds and killed Russell. The sooner I could clear my name, the better.

That evening, I was pleasantly surprised when my brother, Joseph, and his wife stopped by and said they were going with us to the party. They left their car at Azalea Bluff, and the five of us drove out together to Cookie and Cynthia's house. Though it couldn't compare to Big Hal's mansion or even our own home, it was a lovely, two-story place by the water. I'd visited here often with my brother and parents, and memories of us kids running around the yard slid through my mind. Cookie had often come out to play with us until "Cynical" Cynthia would scold him for acting like a child and tell him to come inside. With all three families combined, there was a total of ten of us. We'd had our good times and bad times, but all in all, we'd stood by one another.

My warm feelings of family support soon began to fade away when we walked inside the house and everyone stopped talking to turn around and stare at us. Judging by the looks on their faces, they hadn't expected us to come tonight, and it was apparent that we weren't overly welcome at the party. Big Hal had obviously told Mildred that the diamonds were meant to be a gift for her, and by the hard glare she directed my way, she blamed me for the theft. The Cook's maid, Astrid, stood off to the side with a tray of hors d'oeuvres, looking hesitant and uncertain. Joseph stepped closer and wrapped a supportive arm around my shoulder, and I smiled appreciatively up at my brother.

After a moment of awkward silence, Cookie stepped forward with a broad smile and said in his typical booming voice, "It's about time y'all got here!"

Things started to loosen up after that, but I felt like a stranger in the room full of people I'd grown up with. Brenda waved to me and then turned around to whisper something to Dale Beecher and a couple of her friends.

Just then, one more guest arrived, and I was surprised to see it was Toby Garner. I'd known Toby all my life; he worked with his father as a plumber during the day and volunteered at the fire department three nights a week. What I hadn't realized was that he and Brenda were good enough friends to warrant an invitation to her party. He smiled at me and nodded just before going over to wish Brenda a happy birthday.

After Cookie elbowed Cynthia in the side, she

came over and stiffly thanked us for coming. Her sister, Tammy, who was much sweeter than Cynthia, hurried over to my mother's side and gave her a hug.

"Azalea, I love your dress," she said to me with a kind smile. "Why don't you go on over and join the young people? Dale looks to me like he's feeling a bit out of place tonight."

Nodding, I squared my shoulders and walked across the room toward the small group of young people, stopping along the way to grab a small sandwich from Astrid's tray.

"Did you make these, Astrid?" I asked the pretty young woman. When she nodded, I said, "They're delicious."

When I joined the group, I asked Toby to pour me a glass of punch. He nodded in agreement, and as he hurried off to do my bidding, I stepped up beside Dale Beecher, Big Hal's son. He was twenty-two, quite tall, and ruddy in complexion. He looked down at me with cool, uninterested eyes, not speaking a word.

"As usual, you look like you're enjoying yourself," I quipped.

His expression never changing, he replied, "And as always, you're the center of attention."

I raised my eyebrows. "Don't you mean that Brenda is always the center of attention?" I asked, looking pointedly at the young woman as she and a couple of her friends put a record on and started dancing around the room. Toby returned then with my punch, and I took a long sip of the refreshing drink.

Dale shrugged. "Whatever you say," he replied after Toby walked away. "You know, I'm a little surprised to see you here tonight."

Tilting my head to one side, I asked coolly, "Oh? Did you think I was still in jail?"

Without answering my question, he asked, "How did you manage to get out so quickly?"

I had to force myself not to throw my punch in his face; he'd always been such an arrogant, pompous jerk. Although he wasn't quite bold enough to say so, I could tell he suspected me of stealing his mother's diamonds. If he hadn't stolen them himself, that is. Perhaps it was guilt I was seeing in his eyes instead of blame?

"They released me on bail," I stated. With a doe-eyed expression on my face, I asked softly, "Can you believe they accused me of stealing those diamonds and killing poor Russell?"

Raising one eyebrow, Dale stated drolly, "I'm stunned. Tell me, who do *you* think did it?"

Someone in this room, I thought, but didn't dare say out loud.

With a shrug, I replied, "Probably some stranger who is long gone by now. It happened pretty late, you know. Were you at home?"

"Yes, of course," he replied smoothly. "Where else would I have been that late at night?"

Something about his response made me think he wasn't telling the truth. I needed to find out if he really *was* home, but how? The Beechers had a live-in housekeeper; perhaps I could ask her. *If* she would tell me, that is.

The song changed to a much faster tempo then, and Brenda grabbed me by the hand, pulling me away from Dale. Her eyes were sparkling and her cheeks were rosy with excitement. With a laugh, she cried, "Come on, Azzy, let's show them how to do the Cool Jerk!"

I allowed Brenda to pull me onto the makeshift dance floor, and as the two of us danced, I took in the expressions and reactions of everyone around us. Dale shook his head in disgust and walked from the room. He was right; although I'd never admit it to him, I *did* enjoy being the center of attention. Brenda's male friends whooped and whistled from the sidelines, causing me to laugh. Cynthia and Mildred whispered amongst themselves, and I could tell they were talking about me. Toby watched us with a small smile on his face, and I noticed my sister-in-law murmuring something to my brother. Cookie joined us on the dance floor for a quick moment, causing everyone to laugh as he attempted the silly dance moves.

Just before the music ended, I saw Big Hal motion to Cookie, and they both walked from the room. It seemed they had something important to discuss and didn't wish to be disturbed by the loud music. If what they were discussing was business-related, why wouldn't they ask Papa to join them? I had a feeling the subject of their conversation was something else, something much more serious. What, though, I didn't know, but I intended to find out.

"Thank you, Azzy, for the lovely dance," Brenda said with a laugh as she bowed dramatically from the waist.

"Happy birthday, Brenda," I told her with a smile.

As Brenda hurried over to join Toby, Dale, and the others, I quietly slipped from the room. The hallway was dark, and I could see a sliver of light coming from Cookie's office. Glancing around to make certain no one was lurking about, I slipped closer to the door and listened.

"Do you think he suspects?" Big Hal asked in a low voice.

"No, I don't believe so," Cookie replied. "I think it will be best if we keep our mouths shut and just lie low for a while."

"This could end very badly, you know."

Cookie sighed. "I know, but don't worry. It'll hopefully blow over soon, and we can continue with our plan."

The sound of laughter and approaching footsteps echoed nearby, and I quickly slipped into the shadows beside a large potted plant. Cynthia stepped from the living room and called out for her husband, and the door to the office quickly opened. The men hurried from the room, walking directly past me. I held my breath as they passed, hoping they wouldn't spot me. Once they were gone, I sighed with relief and hurried into the powder room. As I stood before the mirror, staring at my reflection, I replayed the oddly suspicious conversation over in my mind and wondered exactly what the two men had been talking about.

When we arrived back home, it was nearly ten o'clock. After Joseph and Annemarie left, Mama and Papa quickly went to bed. I, on the other hand, was too keyed up after the party to sleep. I read for a little while, and then I went downstairs in search of my purse. When I found it lying on the kitchen table, I opened the magnetic latch to grab my fingernail file but stopped when I noticed a folded piece of paper stuffed into one of the side flaps. With a frown, I pulled the note out and unfolded it, my eyes widening as they scanned across the scrawled handwriting:

Meet me at the old fort tonight at midnight; I have some important information about the robbery and Russell's murder.

CHAPTER 11

Azalea - 1966

I stared at the note in confusion. I hadn't used this purse in several weeks, which meant someone at Brenda's party tonight had to have slipped it inside. Who could it have been? And why did they want to meet at midnight at the old fort, of all places?

I pondered what to do, my mind racing. It would be crazy to go out to that creepy old fort in the middle of the night...wouldn't it?

But what if this is the chance I've been waiting for? I thought.

With a nod, I made my decision. I was going. Spinning around to look at the clock on the wall, I realized with a catch of my breath that I barely had thirty minutes to get there. I hurried quietly through the house and up the stairs to grab a flashlight and a sweater.

I held my breath as I tiptoed back down the stairs and out through the back door, hoping I wouldn't wake my parents. I softly closed the door behind me and hurried through the yard toward the carriage house where my car was parked. As I drove away from the house moments later, I hoped

I wasn't making a mistake.

At only a few minutes 'til midnight, I pulled up to the old fort and sat silently in my car, looking around. A full moon shone brightly from a cloudless sky, its beams casting eerie shadows along the old fortification. The dilapidated stone structure rose from the ground like an ancient monument from the past. Giant oak trees arched overhead, their gnarly branches draped with silvery moss that dangled in the moonlight. I didn't see a soul and wondered if this had been some sort of prank.

Taking a deep breath, I climbed from the car and moved closer to the fort. I could hear the trickling of the river close by, and when the trees overhead suddenly rustled, I jerked in surprise. Glancing up, I shined my flashlight into the branches, my breath catching when a pair of golden eyes glistened back at me. With a loud flapping of its wings, a giant owl flew from the tree and disappeared into the night.

Swallowing past the lump in my throat, I continued walking toward the fort. I could remember hearing the stories of this place when I was a child; stories of how the ghosts of Revolutionary War soldiers roamed the fort at night. I didn't believe in ghosts, but the way the shadows from the moon moved along the bones of the walls made me feel a little edgy.

I reached the arched stone entrance and stopped, listening. The only sounds I could hear were the river and the wind as it whispered softly through the trees. Whisper Island had gotten its name from the Indians who used to roam its sandy shores. According to legend, the Indians had claimed the sound of the breeze from the ocean that rustled through the trees and sea oats was the whisper of their ancestors. Tonight, I could easily believe that.

Suddenly, I thought I saw a shadow moving along the opposite side of the fortification. I froze, my heart catching in my chest. I pressed myself against the wall and squinted, trying to identify if the shadow was human or animal, but it was too dark. Dare I call out? Or perhaps I should quietly move forward in the hope I could see who had left that note in my purse. Did they really just want to share information, or did they intend to do me harm?

I raised my foot to take a step forward when a light suddenly flashed from behind and a voice called out. With a gasp, I spun around, shielding my eyes from the bright light.

"Azalea, is that you?"

The voice belonged to Toby Garner. What was *he* doing here?

"Yes, it's me," I hissed, hurrying toward him. "What are you doing here?"

"I was about to ask you the same question," he replied, eyeing me curiously.

With a sigh, I showed him the note and explained everything. "Now it's your turn," I stated.

"I go on duty tonight in half an hour and was on my way to the fire station," he replied. "I like to drive by this place when the moon is full. I usually don't see people roaming around out here, though."

"Well, I'm sure you scared off whoever was supposed to meet me," I said, feeling irritated.

Taking my arm, Toby said, "I'll look around with you before I go, just in case they're still here."

We searched the entire fort but found no one. Had I really seen a shadow slipping through the darkness? Or had my imagination gotten away with me? Either way, there was no one here now. As Toby and I walked back to our vehicles, I sighed with frustration. Perhaps whoever it was would contact me again.

The next day was Russell's funeral. It had been delayed a few days due to a couple of close family members being out of town. Mama tried to talk me out of going; she knew no one wanted me there. I insisted on attending, however. I would not let rumors and biased hypocrites keep me from saying my final goodbyes to Russell.

As I walked inside the church with my parents, it seemed that every set of eyes turned on me. I could hear the whispers and felt the judgment in their gazes, but I walked to my seat with my head held high. I knew nearly everyone in town was against me and that Russell's family had never approved of me. I wasn't, however, quite prepared for the hate-filled gazes his mother and sister directed my way when they saw me.

"Azalea, don't," Mama whispered, grabbing my arm as I stepped toward the Madison family.

Pulling my arm away, I marched straight up to Russell's mother and said, "I'm sorry for your loss, Mrs. Madison. I hope you can believe me when I say I loved Russell and had nothing to do with his death."

"You've got some nerve," Russell's sister hissed as she stepped between me and her mother. "You always thought you were better than everyone else, especially us poor Madisons. Well, let me tell you this: you're going to prison, Miss Layne. I'll see to that if it's the last thing I do."

With a clenched jaw, I arched one eyebrow and stated coolly, "I'm sorry for *your* loss, too, Ruby. If Russell was still alive, we'd be in-laws. Maybe then you wouldn't hate me so much."

Spinning on my heel, I walked back to my seat and sat down, ignoring all the stares along the way. I couldn't help but hear a few of the whispered comments, though.

"Always bold as brass, that Layne girl."

"She always did have too high of an opinion of herself."

"A little too uppity for someone who's going to prison."

I took a deep breath and let it out slowly as I tried

to rein in my emotions. I hated it here. I hated this island and everyone on it...well, almost everyone. I needed to get away from this viper pit, but how? Russell had been my only hope of escape, but now that he was gone, I was trapped.

CHAPTER 12

Zaylie

The next morning, Alan Whitlock and his construction crew arrived at Azalea Bluff, ready to begin breaking new ground. As Zaylie walked out to show them the new location for the training center, she noticed Rita's handsome foreman, Grady Young, eyeing the spot where Azalea's body was found.

"Ever found a body on the job before?" she asked, smiling as he turned to look at her.

Grady shook his head. "No, ma'am, this was a first." Turning, he pointed to the gravesite and added, "Looks like someone has been out here poking around."

Moving forward to stand next to Grady, Zaylie peered over the police tape and gasped. Freshly dug holes dotted the area all around where the body was discovered. Apparently, someone really *had* been out here the night before!

"I'd better let Sheriff Carter know about this," Zaylie said as a chill raced up her spine. The thought of someone watching her and Smutti from the tree line last night made her skin crawl.

"That old geezer needs a grave of his own," Grady

mumbled.

"I take it you don't think too highly of the old sheriff?" Zaylie asked.

Grady cocked an eyebrow. "My family has never thought too highly of him," he stated.

"You mean because your great-uncle Russell's murder was never solved?" Zaylie questioned.

Grady looked down at her, his handsome face pulled into a scowl. "It could have been if the police department had been more competent," he replied in a hard tone. "Because of everything that happened, my family left the island looking for some closure and a better life. What they found, though, was worse than what they'd left behind."

With those words, Grady turned and stalked away. Zaylie watched him, wondering what he was referring to. She also couldn't tell if he and his family held a grudge only against Odin, or against Azalea as well.

As Whitlock and his crew got to work, Zaylie went inside and reported her findings to Sheriff Carter. His voice sounded tired, and she wondered if filling in for Uncle Bill was turning out to be too much for him. He'd obviously been under a lot of pressure to get it solved over fifty years ago; was he feeling that same pressure again now?

Zaylie had just gotten off the phone when she heard Gran let someone in the front door. Seconds later, the room was filled with the always slightly overwhelming presence of one of the Steele twins.

"Missed me so much that you had to go and tear

a hole in the wall, huh?" Ryker asked when he saw Zaylie, his hazel eyes sparkling.

The man never changes, Zaylie thought.

Deciding to play along, she widened her eyes in mock surprise and asked, "How did you know I did that? And here I thought I'd covered my tracks so well."

Ryker grinned. "You of all people should know it's almost impossible to cover your tracks," he quipped. Leaning over to rub Smutti behind the ears, he asked, "Isn't that right, girl?"

Smutti wagged her tail and looked up at the annoying man with adoring eyes. Pursing her lips, Zaylie refrained from sighing. It seemed that Ryker Steele had a way with females of all shapes and sizes; even ones of the furry variety.

"So, Rita was telling me all about your great aunt," Ryker said, standing up to look at Zaylie. Cocking an eyebrow, he added, "Do you need me to sleep on the sofa again until all of this blows over?"

"Don't you think your girlfriend would have something to say about that?" Zaylie asked drolly. "Besides, Azalea was killed over fifty years ago. I don't think there's any danger now."

The fact that someone had apparently trespassed on their property the night before rang in the back of her mind, but she didn't bring that up. If whoever it was intended to do them harm, they'd have done it last night. Right?

Ryker opened his mouth to say something, but Gran came back into the room and interrupted.

"Sorry about that, dear," she said, "but I had to answer the phone. Zaylie, why don't you show Ryker where the damage has been done?"

"He knows where it is," Zaylie replied. Looking at Ryker, she said, "It's in my bathroom, the same place as before."

"I might need you to show me again," Ryker replied, smiling innocently. "You know how forgetful we men are."

"How you ever made it in the Navy, I'll never know," Zaylie stated in a dry tone.

As they walked up the stairs and into the bathroom, Zaylie was struck by how gutted the wall was. She hadn't been back in here since the Garner men left, and she felt that their work was a bit of overkill.

Ryker whistled when he saw the damage that was done. "This may take a few days to fix," he muttered, stepping forward to take a closer look.

Just then, the tile beneath his foot gave way and Ryker would have fallen if not for his quick reflexes. Out of sheer instinct, Zaylie reached out to grab him, but her foot slipped on the dusty floor and she slammed into Ryker's side. He ended up catching them both, and she found herself pulled tightly against his chest, their faces only inches apart.

"You know, if you wanted to be this close to me, all you had to do was say so," Ryker said in a low tone.

His eyes were teasing but also filled with

something else that made Zaylie's skin tingle. Quickly pulling away, she laughed awkwardly and said, "Sorry about that."

With a smile, Ryker raised an eyebrow and said, "I'm not complaining."

Ignoring his flirtatious comments, Zaylie looked down at the floor and said, "How on earth do you think that tile came loose?"

Ryker shrugged. "It probably happened during the demolition of this wall," he stated. "I'll fix it. By the way, what did you mean earlier by…"

Before he could finish, they were interrupted by the sound of the front door opening and then Gran's voice as she cried, "Why, Dale Beecher, this certainly is a surprise."

Hurrying from the bathroom and down the stairs, Zaylie found a very disgruntled-looking gentleman standing in the foyer. The old man wore a suit and tie, as if he was about to attend a formal gathering.

"Louella," he stated in a stiff voice, "What's this I hear about Azalea's body being found?"

"It's true," Gran said. "It was discovered a few days ago while a construction crew was breaking ground for my granddaughter's new…"

Pointing his finger in her face, Dale interrupted Gran and said, "If those diamonds are found, Louella, I expect to be notified."

Gran squared her shoulders and said tartly, "I hope you don't think they'll be found *here* because Azalea did *not* steal those diamonds!"

His lip curling, Dale asked, "Why was she murdered then?"

Zaylie stepped into the foyer and spoke up. "That's what we're trying to find out, Mr. Beecher," she said. "If those diamonds are found, though, I can assure you that you will be notified...even though I'm sure your family already received the insurance money years ago."

Dale's jaw clenched at Zaylie's statement. "The insurance money has nothing to do with this, young lady," he declared, his southern accent becoming even thicker. There wasn't an "r" to be heard as he continued to rant. "Those diamonds were to become a family heirloom, and I don't appreciate any rude and uncalled-for insinuations coming from the likes of you."

Spinning on his heel, he marched toward the door in a cloud of righteous indignation. With one hand on the doorknob, he turned to look back at Zaylie and said sneeringly, "You look just like her, you know. Let's hope you don't end up like her, too."

Gran gasped, her eyes wide as the older gentleman stomped outside and slammed the door behind him. Looking at Zaylie, she exclaimed, "The nerve of that man! Oh, if only I'd been on my toes, I would have given him a piece of my mind. How dare he barge into our home acting like the king of England? I think I'll just go out there before he leaves and tell him..."

"Don't, Gran," Zaylie quickly said. "The man

basically just threatened me. I don't think we need to press the issue further; at least not until he has had some time to calm down."

With a *tsk,* Gran twisted around and marched into the kitchen without another word. Walking toward one of the large windows on either side of the front door, Zaylie watched Dale Beecher speed away in his Jaguar. She wondered if he'd really meant to threaten her, or if he'd just gotten caught up in the heat of the moment and said more than he intended.

CHAPTER 13

Zaylie

As Grady Young and Alan Whitlock walked around to the front of the house to direct an incoming dump truck, they both spotted Dale Beecher stalking down the front steps toward his car. Judging by the scowl on the man's face, he wasn't very happy.

"What is that all about?" Grady wondered out loud.

"Oh, you know what a tyrant that old man can be," Alan commented.

The two men became quiet as they watched Dale speed away, and Grady began to think about his conversation with Zaylie. He hoped he hadn't said too much. No one knew the real reason he'd moved back to the island, and he didn't want Zaylie to become suspicious and start asking questions. The less people knew, the better.

The dump truck appeared around the curve then, and the two men quickly set about directing him around the house toward the construction site. As they walked that way, Alan couldn't help but look over at the police tape blowing in the wind. He'd spoken with his father after Zaylie's unexpected visit, and his father had shared some very interesting information. Alan had told him not to breathe a word of it to anyone else; he wanted that secret to remain close.

A couple of hours after Dale Beecher left, Rita stopped by, and Zaylie was surprised to see that Shawn Eaton was with her.

"Hi, Shawn," Zaylie greeted their property caretaker. "You did a great job with our shrubs the other day."

"Thanks," he replied with a smile. "I was going to cut the grass behind the house today, but I wanted to make sure it was okay for me to go back there?"

Zaylie nodded. "Yes, just please stay away from the construction crew and the area that's still taped off."

Shawn opened his mouth to ask something else when his phone rang and he stepped outside to answer it.

"Phew, that was a lucky break," Rita stated with a relieved sigh.

Looking at her friend quizzically, Zaylie asked, "What do you mean?"

"Well, Shawn asked if I'd show him the burial site and point out exactly where the body was found, but I was hoping you could do it," Rita replied.

Frowning, Zaylie asked, "Why don't *you* want to show him?"

Flipping a thick, jet-black curl across her

shoulder, Rita replied, "Because Grady is out there. We have a date planned for next weekend, and I don't want him to see me with Shawn."

Zaylie rolled her eyes. "Rita, why are you juggling two guys at once? You ought to be ashamed."

Rita pursed her lips indignantly and hissed, "Shawn and I have been friends for years, you know that, so I'm not *juggling* anyone."

"What's the problem, then?"

"I don't want *Grady* to think I'm juggling anyone," she stated matter-of-factly. When Zaylie gave her a look, she said, "Don't look at me like that. There's nothing wrong with having more than one friend."

With a sigh, Zaylie said, "No, there's not, but I wish you'd at least quit going out with guys you barely know anything about."

"Grady's family is originally from this island, so what more do I need to know about him?" Rita asked.

"I just get the feeling there's something a little strange about him and his family," Zaylie replied with a shrug.

"So? There are some strange people in *my* family, too, but what does that have to do with anything?" Rita asked drolly. "Just look at Ryker."

Laughing, Zaylie had just agreed to walk with Shawn out to the burial site when he rejoined them inside.

"Gran is in the kitchen," Zaylie said to Rita. "Why don't you talk with her for a few minutes while

I walk outside with Shawn? She doesn't need to know what we're doing or she might get upset."

While Rita distracted Gran, Zaylie and Shawn walked out back. Shawn had been the caretaker at Azalea Bluff for nearly a year now; he'd taken over after the last caretaker retired. Zaylie had known him all her life, but the two had always just been casual friends. He was closer in age to her sister, Zoe, so they had never run in the same circles.

"I hope you don't mind that I wanted to see the area everyone in town is talking about," Shawn said with a sheepish smile. "Y'all have become quite the celebrities."

"Gran would not like to hear you say that," Zaylie replied with a chuckle. "She hates that this is happening."

"That's understandable," he said. "I'm sure it brings back unpleasant memories for her."

Zaylie nodded. "It does," she replied. "She and Azalea were best friends."

"So I've heard."

Zaylie wanted to ask what else he'd heard, but they were soon distracted by the excavation site.

"Her body was found right there," Zaylie said, pointing.

Shawn whistled softly. "Wow," he breathed. "Why do you think she was killed? Because someone thought she had the diamonds?"

Zaylie shrugged. "I guess, but it's all a little strange to me," she replied.

"Why is that?" he asked, turning to look at her.

Zaylie crossed her arms, her brow furrowed as she thought. "Well, if she really had those diamonds," she said after a moment, "then whoever killed her would have taken them before shooting her, right?"

"I guess?"

"Then why haven't those diamonds shown back up?" she wanted to know. "If they were sold on the black market, surely at least one piece would have resurfaced somewhere by now."

"So, you think they might be buried out here somewhere?" Shawn asked, looking around the property.

Zaylie shook her head. "No, because I don't think Azalea stole them."

Before the conversation could continue, Sheriff Carter showed up to take a look at the fresh boot tracks on the site. Shawn went on about his work, and by the time Zaylie went back inside, Rita was already gone.

"What did Odin say about the tracks?" Gran asked.

"He made a cast of one print and will come back later to get it," she replied. "He said we need to leave the floodlights on every night and keep a close check on the cameras."

"A lot of good that'll do if someone dangerous is out there, poking around," Gran muttered.

Zaylie's cell phone rang then, and she saw it was Uncle Bill. When she answered, his voice sounded worried.

"Zaylie, old Mr. Peavey wandered off during a family reunion at the park," he said. "His granddaughter just called me; she said they've been searching for over an hour and can't find him. Will you take Smutti out there and see if there is anything y'all can do?"

"Of course," Zaylie immediately replied.

As she changed into a pair of sneakers and grabbed Smutti's lead, her stomach clenched with worry. Mr. Peavey was in his early nineties and had Alzheimer's disease. If he wandered too far away from the park, he could get hit by a car. There was also a lot of marshland in that area, which could cause him to drown if he got stuck in the mud.

"Come on, girl, let's hurry," she said to Smutti, a sense of urgency pushing her to move faster.

CHAPTER 14

Zaylie

When Zaylie arrived at the park, Mr. Peavey's granddaughter, Joan Richards, was on the verge of hysteria. She was the owner of the island's coffee shop and had once been friends with Zaylie's older sister Zoe before she was killed.

"Bill told me you were coming," Joan said as soon as she spotted Zaylie. "I'll take you to the last place we saw him."

As Zaylie and Smutti followed Joan across the park toward a large pavilion with a dozen picnic tables underneath, she went on and on about how she couldn't believe she'd let this happen.

"My husband told me we shouldn't have brought Granddaddy today," she said as tears choked her voice. "I thought it would do him good to get out of the house. I should have at least asked his nurse to come along. I only took my eyes off him for a minute, Zaylie, I promise."

Reaching out to pat the distraught woman's arm, Zaylie said, "Don't worry, Joan, I'm sure we'll find him."

When they stepped beneath the pavilion, Joan

pointed to one of the far tables that was only a few feet away from the tree line.

"He was sitting right there when I went over to speak to Uncle Larry," Joan said.

"Do you have an article of his clothing?" Zaylie asked. "It will help in a place that's been so heavily cross-contaminated."

Nodding, Joan reached into her purse and pulled out a hat. "I brought this along in case he needed it," she said. "I-I didn't want the sun to bother his eyes."

Joan broke down into a sob and collapsed against a nearby picnic table. Zaylie took the hat and said, "It's going to be okay, Joan. Smutti has found dozens of missing people."

She hated to not stay longer and console the poor woman, but every minute counted and she knew she needed to get Smutti on the trail immediately. Leading the dog over to the picnic table where Mr. Peavey had last been seen, she put his hat beneath Smutti's nose and gave her the command to search.

Smutti sniffed around the area for a moment and then headed toward the woods behind the pavilion. After telling Joan to stay behind in case Mr. Peavey returned, Zaylie quickly followed Smutti into the woods.

The ground was solid at first, but the further they went, the closer they got to the river and the ground started to grow softer. Zaylie kept a watchful eye out for water moccasins, as she knew how dangerous it would be if Smutti was bitten. While most snakes would slither away when people were nearby, cottonmouths were bad-tempered and very defensive. They were also highly venomous.

As they wound their way through the dense forest, Zaylie took note of the broken branches and bruised leaves along the ground. Someone had been through here recently, and the further they went, the more concerned Zaylie felt. They were awfully close to the river; what if Mr. Peavey had fallen into the water? With the swift currents, they may never find him.

The trees finally broke, and Smutti paused at the edge of the tree line, her nose to the ground. Zaylie shaded her eyes with one hand as she looked around, taking in their surroundings. Before them was the Savannah River, winding its way through green and golden marshland. It was low tide, which Zaylie was thankful for, and she spotted dozens of fiddler crabs scurrying through the mud. Pelicans and seagulls flew overhead, looking for an afternoon snack, and way out in the water, Zaylie spotted the silver fin of a dolphin.

With a short bark, Smutti turned to the left and ran along the edge of the trees. Zaylie followed, her heart pounding. Would they find Mr. Peavey in time? She always second-guessed herself during searches, wondering if this one would be unsuccessful. Telling family members that you'd been unable to find their loved one was always extremely difficult.

There was a slight curve up ahead, and when they rounded the bend, the sight before her made Zaylie's heart sink. The area was a particularly muddy one, and a slender figure was lying very still in the mud, face up. Smutti barked and started to move forward, but Zaylie stopped her. She didn't want the dog to get stuck in the mud.

Zaylie took off her shoes and hurried forward, her feet sinking into the wet earth and slowing her progress. When she finally reached Mr. Peavey's side, she could see that his eyes were closed and she couldn't tell if he was breathing.

"Mr. Peavey?" Zaylie asked, her voice trembling slightly as she knelt beside him.

Suddenly, Mr. Peavey's eyes popped open and he looked right at her. Startled, Zaylie sat back on her heels and quickly inhaled a breath of salty air.

"Wh-where am I?" Mr. Peavey asked in a weak voice.

Relief flooding over her, Zaylie helped him sit up and said, "Apparently, you decided to take a mud bath."

"How silly of me," he muttered, looking around in confusion.

Zaylie pulled a bottle of water from her pack and offered him a drink. As he sipped the water, she grabbed her cell phone and called Uncle Bill.

"Can you get the rescuers out here?" she asked after sharing their location. "I don't think I can get him out of here by myself."

"Of course," Bill replied. "Good work, honey."

As they sat and waited for the rescuers to find them, Zaylie looked back at Smutti and smiled. Once again, the dog had saved someone's life. She would never know how truly special she was.

That evening, Zaylie, Gran, and Smutti all settled down in the living room to begin their newest nightly routine. A steaming mug of apple cider sat on the table beside the sofa, and as Zaylie opened the old diary, she felt the usual sense of excitement coursing over her.

If I'd known that two days after Brenda Cook's birthday party would be the last day I'd get to spend with my father, I would have told him so many things. I would have said how much I loved him, and how sorry I was for hurting him when I planned to elope with Russell. Why does it feel like life is spiraling out of control? Without Papa, I feel lost and uncertain, and I don't know if I'm going to get through this. I'm afraid Odin will see to it that I go to prison, and I just don't think I could stand that.

I keep replaying the night Papa died over and over in my mind. They said it was an accident, but I'm not so sure...

CHAPTER 15

Azalea - 1966

It was a little after ten o'clock in the evening when I went downstairs to fix myself a warm glass of milk. I felt tense and on edge and knew I needed something to help me relax. When I reached the bottom floor, I noticed Papa's office light was on and I could hear voices coming from inside. Tiptoeing closer, I pressed my ear against the door and listened.

"Do you have to go out so late?" Mama asked, her voice worried. "Why won't you tell me what this is about?"

"Because I don't know if my suspicions are correct," Papa replied. "All I know is that I've seen and heard some very concerning things in the last couple of days, and I need to find out what it all means."

"Why not wait until tomorrow?" Mama wanted to know.

"I've waited long enough; I can't wait any longer," was all he would say.

Mama, in her typical passive manner, didn't ask any more questions. I heard her kiss him goodbye, and then the soft pitter-patter of her footsteps drawing closer to the door. Not wishing them to know I'd been eavesdropping, I spun around and hurried into the kitchen, switching the light on as soon as I entered. I'd just poured some milk into a pan and placed it on the stove when Mama walked in.

"What are you doing, honey?" Mama asked.

"I thought a glass of warm milk might help me relax," I explained. "You haven't been to bed yet?" I asked, nodding my head in the direction of her blue and white polka dot dress, the same one she'd been wearing at supper.

"No, your father and I have been talking," she replied. After a slight hesitation, she added, "He's, uh, going out for a while."

I heard the front door open and shut, and I knew Papa was leaving. I wanted to run after him and ask where he was going, but perhaps when he got back, he would explain what was going on.

The warm milk must have worked, because as soon as my head hit the pillow, I was out like a light. Six hours later, the sound of frantic pounding on the front door awakened me. With bleary eyes, I switched on the lamp by my bed and looked at the clock.

"Four in the morning," I muttered, wondering what was going on.

Pushing myself out of bed, I grabbed my robe and slid it over my shoulders as I hurried from my bedroom and down the stairs. Mama had just reached the foyer; I could see the trembling of her hand as she unlocked and opened the front door.

"Tobias?" I heard her say, and I stepped up behind her to peer over her shoulder.

Toby Garner was standing on the front porch in his fireman uniform. Through the shadows, I could see how tight his expression seemed.

"Mrs. Layne, Azalea," Toby said.

As soon as I heard the tone in his voice, I knew something was wrong. I flipped the foyer light on and opened the door wider, looking out into the dark night. The only vehicle I saw was Toby's car, and I assumed he'd driven here from the station.

"What's wrong, Toby?" I asked, my stomach clenching.

Toby looked at me then, and I immediately knew it was Papa. I waited in silence, my heart pounding with fear.

"I'm sorry to have to tell you this," he said, glancing down at his feet, "but the sheriff asked if I could stop by. He said y'all would need to know as soon as possible."

"Know what, Toby?" Mama asked, her voice shaking.

Taking a deep breath, Toby looked up and said, "It's Mr. Layne. He was involved in a car accident just down the road from here. He didn't make it, Mrs. Layne. I'm so sorry."

I felt the blood leave my face at his words. With a gasp, Mama swayed on her feet and then collapsed into a heap on the floor.

The next day was a blur. Toby carried Mama into the bedroom after she collapsed, and she hadn't risen from her bed or spoken a word since. Odin stopped by just after dawn and explained what had happened.

"It looks like he just ran off the road," he said. "His car hit a tree, and he was pinned inside. It appears that he died instantly."

I was crushed. How could this have happened? *Why* had this happened? I couldn't seem to wrap my head around the fact that Papa was really gone, and I asked to see the body.

"I don't recommend it," Odin told me. "It's pretty banged up. It's him, though, Azalea. Trust me."

I paced around the living room, feeling like my world was spinning out of control. Papa and I had experienced our fair share of problems, but he was the rock of this family and I wasn't sure how we could go on without him.

"Azalea, what was your father doing out so late?"

At Odin's question, I turned to look at him. He was watching me closely, and I had the feeling there was something he wasn't saying. Yet.

"I don't know," I replied. "I heard him and Mama talking last night before he left, but he wouldn't explain where he was going or why. He simply said he'd seen something that had aroused his suspicions and he wanted to see what he could find out."

Odin's forehead wrinkled. "What did he see?" he wanted to know. "And it aroused his suspicions of **what**?"

I shrugged. "I don't know, Sheriff," I stated. "He wouldn't say."

Odin stared at me with a look of doubt in his eyes. Finally, he stood up and said, "Please, give your mother my condolences. I'll see myself out."

Odin left, and I went into the master bedroom to see how Mama was doing. I asked how she was feeling, but she wouldn't speak. She just lay there crying, the mournful sound breaking my heart. Joseph and Annemarie stopped by and tried to get her to come into the kitchen to eat breakfast, but it was like she couldn't hear us.

"If she hasn't eaten anything by tomorrow morning, call the doctor," my brother told me, his face pulled taunt.

"I will," I replied, nodding.

"I'm so sorry about Papa Layne," Annemarie said as tears filled her pale blue eyes. "It's hard to believe he's really gone."

I hugged them both, my heart heavy. I was glad to not have to go through this alone, but I knew Joseph was torn up about losing Papa. The two had a falling out when Joseph decided to become a lawyer instead of filling his father's shoes at the bank, and I knew he regretted it now. They'd managed to patch things up, but it had never really been the same after that.

"We'll talk about funeral arrangements later," Joseph told me, giving me a kiss on the cheek just before they left.

They'd only been gone half an hour when my best friend, Louella, stopped by. I'd called her earlier to tell her what happened, but she hadn't been home so I left a message. Lou was like a sister to me, and I knew she loved my parents as if they were her own. She was engaged to be married and I hadn't seen as much of her lately, but I understood that. One can't expect things to remain the same forever.

"Oh, Azalea," Lou said as soon as I opened the front door, her eyes red and face splotchy.

We cried in each other's arms for what felt like hours. Papa was the only real father Louella had ever known, and her heart was shattered over his loss. We sat in the living room and talked about what happened and the memories we shared of him.

"How is Mama Layne?" Lou asked.

I sighed. "She hasn't budged from her bed all day," I said. "She won't eat or drink. Joseph said if this continues through the night, I'll need to call the doctor in the morning."

"The poor thing," Lou said, shaking her head. "Could I go see her?"

I nodded and followed her into Mama's room. I stood in the doorway and watched with surprise as Mama reached for Louella as soon as she saw her. Lou held her tightly and the two cried for several minutes, and then she managed to convince Mama to drink some water. Mama never spoke a word; she simply nodded her head as a way of acknowledgment. I'd called her sister, Aunt Maggie, that morning and she'd said she could be here tomorrow. Hopefully, she would have the same effect as Louella and be able to help her.

I walked Lou out to her car and gave her another hug. After promising I'd call if I needed anything, I waved goodbye and watched as she drove away. Seeing her car grow smaller and smaller in the distance and then finally disappear around the bend was almost like a metaphor to me. It seemed that everyone I loved and life as I knew it was slowly disappearing.

With a heavy sigh, I turned and went inside. I stood quietly in the foyer for a moment, my eyes drifting toward Papa's office. I felt my feet begin to move in that direction, and a moment later, I found myself rummaging through his desk. What I expected to find, I wasn't sure, but after going through all the drawers and papers on top, I hadn't found a thing. Blowing out a frustrated breath, I sat down in his chair and rubbed my aching temples.

The clock on Papa's desk chimed, and I looked to see that it was after 5:00 p.m. My eyes then drifted over to the stack of books next to the clock, and I noticed there was a small book tucked away between the larger ones. When I pulled it out, I realized it was Papa's daily pocket planner.

He usually kept it with him and I wondered why he'd left it here. Opening the little book, I turned to the last written page and looked over the day's notes. Most of the day held meetings with clients, but after his lunch break, there was an odd note written. It said:

Go talk to A and check out my theory.

I stared at the note in confusion. Who was "A" and what was Papa's theory? I then glanced to the bottom of the page, and my eyes widened.

After talking to A, my suspicions were confirmed. I'm going back tonight to find out more.

I closed the book and tucked it into my pocket, my mind racing. I had to find out where Papa went yesterday, and I had to figure out who "A" was.

CHAPTER 16

Zaylie

T hat was such a hard time," Gran commented softly as Zaylie closed the diary. "I loved Azalea's parents dearly; they were the parents I never had, you know. I was truly heartbroken by everything that happened."

"I'm so sorry," Zaylie said gently. "That must have been terrible for all of you. Where were *your* parents, Gran? I've heard you talk about them before, but you never gave many details."

Glancing away, Gran sighed and said, "I suppose it's high time you knew the truth about my side of the family." After taking a deep breath, she began. "My father was an alcoholic. He had a terrible temper when he was drinking. I remember Mama sending me over to Azalea's many a night because she knew he would become violent and she didn't want me to be around to see it." Her eyes glazed over a bit, and she added softly, "He never hit me; only Mama. She'd cover the bruises and act like everything was okay, but I knew how badly she was hurting. When I was fifteen, Mama got cancer and Dad left. Mama struggled off and on for over four years before the cancer finally won."

Tears slowly slipped down Zaylie's face as she listened to the pain in Gran's voice. She'd never known the heartaches this woman had faced in her lifetime, but in that moment, she loved and respected her more than ever.

"Azalea's parents were always so kind to us and also to me," Gran said as she pulled a tissue from her pocket and blew her nose. "They were what I always wanted my own parents to be like, and in a way, they took me in as a second daughter. They helped pay many of Mama's doctor's bills, and I remember how Mother Layne would drop off a casserole or something for supper at least once a week after my father left. I don't know how we would have made it without them."

"Is that why you wanted to live here after Gramp died?" Zaylie asked.

Gran nodded. "Yes," she replied with a soft smile. "Plus, you and Zoe were raised here until...well, you know. I can picture you both sliding down the staircase and running through the grass in your bare feet. This old place holds so many wonderful memories."

Zaylie smiled in agreement. Scooting closer to her grandmother, she wrapped an arm around her shoulders and said warmly, "Thank you for telling me all of this, Gran. I don't know how you managed to become such a wonderful mother and grandmother with everything you went through, but you're the absolute best, and I hope you know that."

Gran started to cry again, and she leaned over to kiss Zaylie's cheek. "Thank you, honey. I love you so much."

They both went to bed soon after, but Zaylie couldn't stop thinking about what Gran told her. How awful it must have been to be raised by an abusive father and then to watch your mother slowly die. Zaylie's heart broke for Gran, but after hearing her story, she felt closer to her now more than ever.

The next day, Zaylie and Gran drove out to Brenda Cook's place. She was "Cookie" and Cynthia's only daughter. Her name was Brenda Johnson now, but her husband died a few years ago. According to Gran, she'd never had children and lived alone. She and Gran had loosely stayed in touch all these years but rarely saw each other.

"Her husband must have made a good living," Zaylie commented as they parked in front of the huge two-story house.

"He was a lawyer," Gran replied. "Actually, he was Azalea's lawyer."

Zaylie looked at Gran in surprise. "Lloyd Johnson was Brenda's husband?"

Gran nodded. "That's right. They got married a couple of years after Azalea disappeared."

The two stepped from Zaylie's car, climbed up the dozen or so stairs that led to the front door, and rang the doorbell. After a moment, a woman who was a couple of years younger than Gran opened the door. She was dressed to the T, as if she was expecting company, but Zaylie guessed she always looked that way. Her skin was soft and smooth with hardly any wrinkles, and her eyes were bright and piercing.

"Louella Ferguson, is that you?" she asked in a soft, Southern drawl.

Gran smiled and nodded. "It's good to see you, Brenda," she greeted the woman. "This is my granddaughter, Zaylie. I hope we're not disturbing you?"

Brenda turned her piercing gaze to Zaylie and looked her up and down. "My goodness, you look so much like dear Azzy," she breathed. "Doesn't she, Louella?"

"She certainly does," Gran agreed.

"Dear me, where are my manners?" Brenda *tsked*, waving a hand in the air as she opened the door wider. "Please, come in."

She led them into a beautifully decorated parlor with antique furniture, spotless silver, and a Turkish silk rug. An older gentleman sat in one of the chairs, and despite his age, he quickly sprang to his feet when the women entered.

"My, my, if I'd known I'd be surrounded by such lovely ladies, I'd have brought my harmonica," he quipped boisterously.

Gran and Zaylie laughed while Brenda shook her head. "You silly man," she said, swatting at him. "Louella, you remember my good friend, Gerry, don't you?"

Gran cocked an eyebrow and said teasingly, "How could I forget him? He was always such a flirt."

Gerry threw back his head and guffawed loudly. "Louella Ferguson, I knew I should have called on you after hearing your husband had passed," he stated, wiggling his eyebrows. "You were the one that got away, you know."

By the annoyed expression on her face, it seemed that Brenda didn't care about the way the conversation was going. "Why don't you all sit down?" she asked, interrupting Gerry.

After everyone took a seat, Gran said, "I'm sorry to just pop by like this, but I'm sure you've heard about our situation."

"About Azalea?" Gerry asked with a chuckle. "Everyone in town is talking about it."

Giving Gerry a look, Brenda said, "Yes, Louella, we've heard."

"My granddaughter and I are trying to figure out what could have happened," Gran said, glancing over at Zaylie. "Can you remember any particular details of those awful days when Azalea was accused of stealing those diamonds?"

Taking a sip of tea, Brenda said, "It was so long ago, Louella, that I'm not sure I remember much about it except what a scandal it was."

"So, you don't have any idea who the real thief could have been?" Zaylie asked.

Gerry raised his eyebrows in surprise. "Didn't

they prove that Azalea did it?"

"No, they didn't," Gran stated matter-of-factly.

Eyeing Gerry, Brenda cleared her throat and said, "Louella never believed that, Gerry."

I thought she didn't remember much about it, Zaylie thought.

"We believe someone else did it," Zaylie said, "and Azalea found out about it, which is probably why she was killed."

Tapping her chin, Brenda said, "You know, I believe I *do* remember something odd."

Gran, Zaylie, and Gerry all leaned toward her in anticipation, waiting to see what she had to say.

"I can't recall everything that was said, but I bumped into her a couple of days before she disappeared," she said. "She was very pale and seemed to be in a hurry. I remember thinking she acted as if she was very worried about something."

"Where did this take place?" Zaylie wanted to know.

"At the police station, of all places," she replied. "Odin asked Dale and me to stop by; he had some questions to ask us about our whereabouts the night of the robbery. We both arrived at the same time and as we were walking through the parking lot to go inside, we ran into Azalea as she was leaving. She said Odin had a few questions to ask her, and she seemed quite anxious to leave."

"Did you notice if anyone followed her out of the parking lot?" Zaylie asked.

Brenda shook her head. "I'm afraid not."

Silence filled the room for a moment as everyone thought about what Brenda had said. Finally, Gerry broke the silence with a bombshell statement.

"Surely, y'all ought to be able to piece all of this together with that diary or whatever it is that you have."

Both Gran and Zaylie's mouths dropped open. They stared at Gerry for a moment, completely speechless, until Gran finally cleared her throat and asked how he knew about the diary.

Reaching up to pat her short, gray curls, Brenda gave Gerry a look and said, "Oh, it's been going around town, Louella."

"It's just an old diary that we keep among the family," Gran stated in a pointed tone. Standing, she forced a tight smile and said, "Well, we'd best get going. Thank you so much, Brenda, for allowing us to pop by like this."

Waving a hand in the air, Brenda said graciously, "Y'all are welcome anytime."

As Zaylie and Gran left the house, Gran was seething. "Who on earth told them about that diary?" she ranted as they drove away. Looking over at Zaylie, she asked, "Did you tell Rita about it?"

Zaylie shook her head. "No, but it **was** lying on the kitchen counter when she and Shawn stopped by yesterday. Maybe they noticed? I can't imagine that Rita would tell anyone about it, though, without prying me with questions first."

Gran tapped her fingers against the passenger door, her lips pursed with irritation as she thought. After a moment, she said, "Chase and Toby also saw it when they came into the kitchen the other day, and Chase was acting very nosy about it."

Zaylie sighed. "Do you think Odin will demand to see it?"

With a huff, Gran stated, "I don't care if he does or not, he's not getting his hands on that diary. And if he brings a warrant, then I have a feeling the diary will suddenly become lost."

Zaylie laughed. Gran had a strong dislike for Sheriff Carter, but Zaylie knew old prejudices ran deep. He'd accused someone she cared about of being a thief and murderer, and according to Azalea's diary, he'd hounded her until she was killed. In Zaylie's opinion, he'd handled the whole situation badly, and he wasn't doing any better of a job now.

As they turned onto Azalea Bluff, the gray skies opened up and rain began to beat against the car. Zaylie moaned, as she knew this would mean the construction crew would, once again, have to stop working. Would she ever get this training center built?

Brenda watched from the window as Zaylie and Louella drove away.

This could become a problem, she thought as a

feeling of worry niggled in the back of her mind.

It seemed that the two women were very determined to dig up old bones from the past. Hopefully, Azalea's would be the only ones they found. Still, she wondered if she should take a few extra precautions. Just in case.

CHAPTER 17

Zaylie

That night, Zaylie settled onto the sofa while she waited for Gran to get out of the shower. The rain had finally stopped, but the freshly dug ground in the backyard was muck and mud. Mr. Whitlock called and said they wouldn't be able to return for a couple of days, and Zaylie tried not to feel discouraged.

Smutti had just settled down on the floor at Zaylie's feet when she suddenly stood back up and began to growl. Zaylie looked down at the dog, her skin tingling at the way Smutti's stark white teeth glistened in the lamp's light as she faced the door and snarled.

"What is it, girl?" Zaylie whispered.

Suddenly, the siren from the security system began to sound, echoing loudly throughout the house. With her tail down, Smutti let out a ferocious bark and took off like a rocket from the room. Her heart pounding, Zaylie hurried after her, wondering what on earth was going on. Was someone in the house?

"Zaylie!" Gran cried in a panicked voice, and Zaylie's heart dropped.

Smutti was running toward the kitchen, but Zaylie rushed to her grandmother's room. She'd just thrown the master bedroom door open when the shattering of glass sounded. Seconds later, the alarm shut off and the house was flooded in darkness.

Blinking, Zaylie stopped for a moment, trying to get her bearings. The house had become eerily silent, but her ears still rang from the piercing security siren.

"Gran, are you okay?" she called out in a breathless tone.

"I'm in the bathroom," Gran cried. "The toilet is overflowing and I can't see a thing. What is going on?"

Shaking her head in an attempt to clear it, Zaylie hurried into the dark bedroom. She fumbled along the bedside table for a flashlight but couldn't find one. With a moan of frustration, she gave up and rushed into the bathroom. She could hear the toilet running and immediately could tell she was walking through water as she made her way toward the toilet.

"Gran, since you're near the window, open the shade," Zaylie said, her voice echoing in the room. "Maybe the moon will cast enough light in here for us to see."

In a matter of seconds, the shade was lifted, and through the dim shadows, Zaylie was able to get the water to the toilet shut off. Water covered the bathroom floor and was already drifting into the bedroom, but Zaylie couldn't worry about cleaning it up just yet. Right now, she had to find Smutti and figure out what was going on.

Just then, the sound of thumping could be heard coming from the direction of the kitchen. Zaylie froze, her heart kicking into overdrive. She hadn't heard Smutti bark or the sound of her paws tapping along the hardwood floors in some time. Where was she?

"Gran, I think someone may be in the house," Zaylie whispered. "Where is your cellphone?"

"I don't know," Gran replied, her voice trembling. "In the kitchen, maybe?"

"What about your flashlight?" Zaylie asked.

"It's in the drawer beside my bed, but the batteries are almost dead."

"Okay, stay here," Zaylie told her as she carefully made her way across the slick, wet floor and into the bedroom.

The room was pitch black as Zaylie felt around the drawer beside Gran's bed. When her fingers finally landed on the tiny flashlight, she breathed a sigh of relief. She clicked it on and her heart sank. The beam was very faint and flickering, and she knew it wasn't going to last much longer.

The thumping in the kitchen could still be heard, and as Zaylie stepped quietly into the foyer, she grabbed an old iron candlestick from the foyer table. She glanced toward the staircase, wondering if she should run upstairs for her phone, but she knew the intruder would hear her, and she didn't want to leave Gran alone downstairs.

Suddenly, Zaylie heard the **whooshing** sound of the kitchen's swinging door and she froze. Quickly, she switched off the flashlight, pressed herself into a corner, and waited. Slow, measured footsteps drew closer and closer, and Zaylie could see the faint beam of a flashlight along the floor. She feared that if her heart pounded any harder, she might faint. Should she call out? Or wait until he was close enough to bash him over the head?

She could see his silhouette now but couldn't make out any discernable features. He had his hand over the beam of the flashlight, blocking most of the light, but she could see that it was a man. When he reached the entrance to the living room, he stopped, and Zaylie held her breath. If he moved his hand from the light and shined it around the room, he'd see her standing in the corner. What would he do? Surely, he knew there were people in the house. The fact that he was acting so boldly told Zaylie that she needed to keep as still and quiet as possible. Where was Smutti? Had he hurt her?

He suddenly turned then and walked into the living room. Zaylie waited for a moment, listening. She could hear the floorboards creaking beneath his feet, and then there was the sound of shuffling and bumping. It sounded as if he was looking for something.

And then it hit her. He was looking for Azalea's diary! Zaylie remembered leaving it lying on the sofa when she left the room only a few minutes before. Would he spot it? What would she do if he took it?

Taking a deep breath, Zaylie eased forward. She had to know who was in her house, and she clutched the candlestick tighter in her hand as she neared the living room. The closer she came, the more her heart raced. When she reached the opening, she peered around the doorway to see that his back was to her. He was on the far side of the room, ruffling through the books on the bookshelf. With a trembling hand, Zaylie slowly raised the tiny flashlight and pointed it at him. She clicked the button, but nothing happened, and her heart nearly stopped when he spun around and aimed his light directly into her face.

"Wh-what do you want?" she asked in a shaking voice.

Before he could utter a word, Zaylie heard the master bedroom door swung open.

"Zaylie? What's going on?" Gran yelled.

Dropping the book he held in his hand, the man rushed toward her, clicking off his flashlight in the process. With a gasp, Zaylie stumbled backward, the candlestick raised high in the air. It was dark and the spots in her eyes from the flashlight prevented her from seeing him, but she could hear the pounding of his footsteps as he drew closer.

"Gran, go back into your room!" Zaylie cried. With Gran's bad eyes, Zaylie didn't know how on earth she had managed to make it from the bathroom all the way into the foyer, but it terrified her to think of what this man might do to a defenseless old lady.

An elbow grazed Zaylie's arm just then, and she swung her weapon blindly in the darkness. She missed her target, and she could feel the rush of air as he ran past her and back through the kitchen. Thoughts raced wildly through her mind, but Zaylie did the only thing she could think to do at that moment; she ran upstairs in search of her phone. She hadn't considered the fact that she might break her neck in the pitch-black darkness, but after only a couple of missteps and a few bumps on her arms and ankle, she finally located her phone.

As Zaylie dialed 9-1-1, she hurried back down the stairs to ensure that Gran was all right. When the operator answered and Zaylie told her what happened, she said an officer would be at the house in minutes.

"Gran, are you okay?" Zaylie asked when she found her grandmother hiding behind the bedroom door with an umbrella clutched in her hands.

"Y-yes," Gran stuttered, her eyes wide. "What happened?"

"I don't know exactly, but I've got to find Smutti," Zaylie replied as she opened the gate to their property through an app on her phone.

Gran reached out and grabbed her arm. "Honey, wait until the police get here. Please."

It was killing Zaylie to not know where her dog was, but it was obvious that Gran was scared to death and she couldn't leave her alone. As soon as she heard the sirens, though, she told Gran to let the police in before she rushed through the house, calling Smutti's name.

Zaylie raced into the kitchen, stopping in her tracks as she shined her phone's flashlight around and took in the mess. A shattered cookie jar lay on the floor near the counter, and it was apparent that every drawer had been searched. The back door stood wide open, and Zaylie was just beginning to wonder if Smutti was somewhere outside when she heard a whine coming from the direction of the garage.

Hurrying toward the garage door, Zaylie swung it open and was immediately greeted by slobbery kisses and a wagging tail. Her eyes filling with tears of relief, Zaylie kneeled down and hugged Smutti. She then ran her hands over her large body, making certain there were no cuts or broken bones.

"It looks like he shoved you out here and locked the door," Zaylie muttered as Smutti continued to whine and prance around.

Zaylie stood and shined her phone's flashlight around the garage, taking note of the breaker box that stood open. Apparently, the intruder had broken into the house, run into the garage, flipped the main breaker, and then managed to outsmart Smutti by locking her outside. Zaylie couldn't understand why he would risk such a thing when two women and a dog lived in the house. Maybe he'd thought they were out? Whatever the reason, Zaylie fought back a chill of foreboding that raced over her body. A man had broken into their house that night, which meant someone was getting desperate to either find the diamonds or that diary.

CHAPTER 18

Zaylie

J ust as Zaylie was about to explain what happened to the young rookie police officer, Uncle Bill called.

"Put me on speakerphone so I can hear what's going on," he told her.

Zaylie did as he asked and then proceeded to tell both men what happened.

"Did you recognize the man?" the officer asked.

Zaylie shook her head. "I could only make out his shadow and nothing more," she replied.

"Could you tell how old he was?" Bill spoke up.

"By the way he carried himself and the swift way he ran out of here, I'd say he was no older than forty," Zaylie said.

"By the way you describe him, I doubt he's much older than you," Bill stated.

"Why break in when we're at home?" Zaylie wanted to know. "That seems so brazen."

"Perhaps he was hired by someone to run in and grab something in particular, which would explain why he left so quickly without attacking you. He wasn't looking for a fight." Bill hesitated. "Zaylie," he continued in a serious tone. "I've heard the rumors around town about Azalea's diary. Is it true?"

Zaylie and Gran gave each other a look. When they realized the officer was watching them carefully, they both cleared their throats and looked away.

"Let's just assume that whoever it was simply came here on a treasure hunt," Zaylie said, clearly avoiding the question.

Bill sighed. "He was looking for the diamonds, you mean?"

"Right," she replied. Glancing at the officer, she asked, "Could you arrange to have a police car parked out front tonight? Gran and I are a little on edge after what's happened."

Bill spoke to the young officer, who readily agreed to stay. As he went back outside to his cruiser, Bill asked Zaylie if she'd checked the security cameras.

"I'll check now," she replied, quickly opening the app on her phone. After a moment, she sighed with frustration and said, "He threw mud on the camera at the back door, so the only thing all the other cameras picked up was someone dressed in black slinking around in the shadows."

"I'm assuming he must have climbed the stone fence to get onto your property, which supports my theory that he's a younger man," Bill stated. "Look, I know you don't want to talk about the diary, but y'all had better make sure it's hidden away in a safe place tomorrow when Odin comes by."

"Thanks, Uncle Bill," Zaylie said sweetly before hanging up.

"Until we get this business settled, the security system stays turned on at all times," Gran stated as she marched over to the panel by the door and punched in the code. "I've never before in my life had someone break into my home, and if the lights had been on where I could have seen what I was doing, that man would have wished he'd chosen any other house but this one to break into!"

"I'm just glad he didn't hurt either of us *or* Smutti," Zaylie replied. Glancing at the grandfather clock, she added with a sigh, "Come on, we need to clean up all that water in your bathroom. I have a feeling it's going to be a long night."

The next morning, Mr. Garner and Chase came out to the house to see about the issue with the toilet. After a thorough investigation, it was determined that the septic tank needed to be pumped.

"I can recommend a really good company in Savannah," Toby said. Looking at Gran, he added, "Your toilet is also leaking, Louella."

"Oh, dear," Gran moaned. "Can you fix it, Toby?"

"I honestly think it needs to be replaced," he replied. "If you'd like, Chase can pick one up for you and we'll get it installed tomorrow."

129

Gran agreed, and as Chase pulled up a few different toilets online for her to look at, Zaylie decided to ask Toby a few questions.

"Mr. Toby, did you used to be a firefighter?" she asked, smiling at the older gentleman.

Toby nodded. "I sure was, young lady."

"Were you working the night Azalea's father was killed?" Zaylie asked, although she already knew the answer.

Toby hesitated, tilting his head to the side as he thought. "Yes, as a matter of fact, I was," he replied. "Goodness, I hadn't thought of that in years, but now that you brought it up, I can remember how terrible that was."

"What exactly happened?" she wanted to know. "Gran doesn't remember much about it."

Toby reached up and scratched at his thin, wispy white hair. "His car was all smashed up against a tree," he replied with a faraway look in his eyes. "I remember noticing a dent on the left side of his bumper, which I thought was unusual. When I pointed it out to Odin, though, he brushed me off."

Zaylie's eyes widened. "You think someone ran him off the road?" she asked.

Toby shrugged. "I sort of wondered about it, but Odin said I shouldn't spread that around, so I never told anybody until now."

The front door swung open then, and Ryker stepped inside, interrupting the conversation. Toby announced that he had to get to another job and said he'd return the next day to install the new toilet. While Chase and Gran continued to talk, Ryker asked Zaylie what was going on. After she'd explained the events of the night before, he was wide-eyed with shock.

"You didn't get a look at the guy at all?" he wanted to know.

Zaylie shook her head. "Unfortunately, it was too dark."

Gran and Chase joined them in the foyer, and Chase said he was leaving to go pick up the new toilet. As Zaylie walked him out, she asked how he liked working with his grandfather.

"It's okay," he replied nonchalantly. "I never figured to become a plumber, and if it means working until I'm an old man, I'm not sure how long I'll stick with it."

"I thought Mr. Garner continued to work because he enjoys it, not because he has to," Zaylie stated, wondering if the family was hurting for money.

Chase cut his blue eyes over at Zaylie, and for a moment, she thought she saw something reflected in the depths of his gaze. She couldn't be entirely certain, but it seemed he wanted to say something important, but then changed his mind. His expression turned neutral, and he simply smiled and shrugged his broad shoulders.

"Yeah, I guess so," he replied. "See y'all tomorrow."

Once he was gone, Zaylie went back inside and announced that she wanted to go talk to Dale

Beecher.

"After the way he acted the other day?" Gran asked in disbelief.

"I need to ask him some questions," Zaylie replied. "Do you know where he lives?"

"I think he and his wife moved to one of those fancy penthouses a few years ago," Gran replied. "You'll have to call first before stopping by."

Gran called Brenda Cook-Johnson and got Dale's number, but she refused to call Dale or even go with Zaylie to see him.

"I never could stand that man when we were young," she stated indignantly, "and I have no desire to see him again now after the way he acted the other day."

With a sigh, Zaylie called the man and spoke with his wife.

"I just got back from a cruise," she said in a high-pitched, nasal voice, "and I'm so worn out that I just booked an appointment at the spa. Come on by in about an hour, honey. Dale will be here then."

"I don't think you should go alone," Gran said as soon as Zaylie ended the call. "Not after the way he threatened you."

"Come with me then," Zaylie said.

Pursing her lips, Gran said matter-of-factly, "Oh, like *I* would be able to protect you if something happened." Glancing at Ryker, she smiled sweetly and asked, "Why don't you take Ryker with you?"

"Gran, I don't think…"

"I would love to go," Ryker interrupted, his eyes

twinkling. "I'll head upstairs and get a bit of work done, and whenever you're ready to go, just let me know."

As he hurried upstairs, whistling a happy tune, Zaylie gave Gran a look.

"Is **this** the real reason you wouldn't agree to go see Dale?" she asked, crossing her arms. "You planned to ask Ryker to go with me all along?"

With an innocent expression, Gran said, "Don't be ridiculous. You have to agree, though, that an ex-military man with all those big muscles would do a much better job of protecting you than I would."

With that being said, Gran turned and hurried toward the kitchen. Zaylie sighed and shook her head, wondering if her grandmother would ever stop trying to set her up.

An hour later, Zaylie and Ryker arrived at the building where the Beechers lived. The place was four stories high and used to be a single-family dwelling until it was turned into luxury apartments a few years ago. After speaking with the maid over the intercom, the downstairs door was opened for them to enter.

"You'll have to use the old service elevator, as our regular one is under repair," she told them.

When they stepped into the foyer and Zaylie saw how tiny the service elevator was, she said, "I'd rather use the stairs."

Glancing at her curiously, Ryker stated, "I think the stairs are all the way at the back of the building." Grabbing her hand, he pulled her toward the elevator and said, "Come on, it's only four stories; it won't take long."

They stepped into the tiny room, which was barely big enough for the two of them, and Zaylie focused on controlling her breathing. Ever since the night she was locked in that dark closet when her sister was kidnapped, she'd hated tight spaces. As the door closed and the elevator started to move slowly upward, she closed her eyes and told herself it wouldn't be long.

Just a few more seconds...you can do this...

Suddenly, the elevator stopped and the lights flickered. Zaylie's eyes popped open and she looked around, wondering what was going on. They hadn't arrived at Dale's penthouse yet; they'd barely climbed two stories.

Just when Zaylie looked up and noticed the look of concern on Ryker's face, the tiny little elevator shuddered slightly and everything went black.

CHAPTER 19

Zaylie

Zaylie glanced wildly about, trying to get her bearings in the darkness. The elevator was eerily still and silent, and Zaylie could hear no alarms or sirens going off.

"What in the world?" Ryker mumbled, and she could hear him patting something. "Zaylie, do you have your cell phone? I must have left mine at your house."

Zaylie swallowed past the dry lump in her throat and said in a raspy voice, "N-no. I left mine in your truck."

"Well, this is great," he replied, sighing. "The men working on the other elevator must have hit something. It'll probably turn back on in a few minutes."

They were stuck...in a tiny elevator...in the dark. Zaylie could feel the air already becoming thick and heavy. Would they die in here? What if they couldn't get them out in time?

Spots danced before her eyes, her heart was pounding out of control, and she was starting to feel lightheaded. A panic attack was coming on; she hadn't had one in years, but she knew the signs. Reaching out with a trembling hand, she groped through the darkness until she found Ryker's arm.

"I-I can't b-breathe," she gasped.

She felt him turn toward her, and as her eyes began to adjust to the darkness, she could vaguely make out his large silhouette.

"Zaylie, are you claustrophobic?" he asked in a worried tone.

"Y-yes," she rasped.

Putting his arm around her, Ryker began to rub her back as he said, "It's okay, Zaylie. Take a deep breath and let it out slowly."

As she did what he said, she could feel his warm breath on her forehead and found it to be oddly comforting somehow. He took her hand, and she squeezed it with shaking fingers as spasms threatened to overtake her.

"Close your eyes and imagine an open field," he said, and Zaylie did just that. "The sky is blue, the birds are singing, and the air is cool."

Zaylie clung to the soothing sound of his deep, rumbling voice as he talked, forcing herself to focus on what he was saying instead of the racing of her heart. After a few moments, she finally felt herself begin to relax, and she wished desperately for a cool drink of water.

"Feeling better?" he asked.

Zaylie nodded, although he couldn't see her. "Yes, thank you," she said softly.

"Good, I was hoping to distract you; I'm glad it worked." After a slight hesitation, he added in a devilish voice, "If it hadn't, I was planning to kiss you next; that would have snapped you out of it."

Zaylie's eyes popped open, and she felt her face flush. "I believe one unpermitted kiss from you is quite enough," she replied tartly.

"Unpermitted? I seem to remember that you *wanted* that kiss," he shot back.

Zaylie rolled her eyes. "I was a kid, and I thought you were someone else," she retorted. "How typical of you to wear the same Halloween costume as Micah and not bother to tell me it was *you* behind that mask instead of him."

Ryker chuckled. "Ah, yes, you always did have a thing for Pierce, didn't you?" Moving a little closer, he slowly slid his fingers up her arm and said in a low voice, "Maybe I wanted to be your first kiss... and maybe I also want to be your last."

Zaylie's heart rate kicked back into overdrive, but this time, it had nothing to do with her claustrophobia. He was standing so close that she could smell the faint, woodsy scent of his aftershave, and the way her skin tingled beneath his touch made her question her sanity. When he leaned forward and touched his lips to her temple, she wasn't sure if she wanted to slap him or pull him closer.

Before she could do either, the lights suddenly switched on and the elevator roared back to life with a jerk. Zaylie quickly stepped away from Ryker, bumping her shoulder painfully against the wall in the process. He grinned at her but didn't say anything, and she wondered why the air suddenly felt so warm.

Probably because the electricity was off and there's hardly any ventilation in here, she told herself.

When they made it to the top floor, Zaylie all but dove from the elevator as soon as the door slid open. She patted her hair and straightened her shirt, all the while avoiding Ryker's gaze.

"Ready?" he asked as he raised a hand to ring the doorbell.

Zaylie nodded, and within seconds, they were ushered into an immaculate and spacious apartment by the maid. The woman led them into the living room, and Zaylie soaked in the breathtaking views of the ocean that glistened just past the floor-to-ceiling windows.

"Yes, Miss Layne?"

Zaylie turned to see the elderly gentleman wearing an expensive suit and ascot. His white hair was slicked back, and a white mustache graced his top lip. She hadn't gotten much of an opportunity to observe him before, but it was clear to see that he was a very wealthy man.

"Hello again, Mr. Beecher," she replied. "I'm sorry for stopping by like this. I'd also like to apologize for offending you the other day. We've been under somewhat of a strain lately, and I let my temper get the better of me."

He nodded coolly and motioned toward the leather sofa. When they took their seats, Zaylie introduced Ryker. Mr. Beecher barely acknowledged him; his steely gray eyes stayed steadily on Zaylie as he studied her with one critical, raised eyebrow.

"You have a beautiful place here," Zaylie said with a polite smile.

"Yes, I know," was his short reply.

Clearing her throat, Zaylie said, "Mr. Beecher, do you remember anything about what happened all those years ago when the bank was robbed?"

With smooth, manicured fingers, Mr. Beecher pulled a cigar from his pocket and lit it with a match. After puffing silently for a moment, he finally nodded and said, "Yes, I remember it like it was yesterday. I always knew Azalea's life would end badly."

Zaylie tilted her head questioningly. "Oh? Why is that?"

Mr. Beecher's silver gaze never wavered as he said in a rather monotone, uninterested voice, "She always had to be the center of attention. She was spoiled and beautiful, and she always got what she wanted. She used people and never cared whether she hurt them or not."

Zaylie didn't quite know what to say. Dale Beecher was a very unusual man. While at their house, he'd been irate and almost out of control. Now, however, he seemed to be very cold and cynical, and yet he was accusing her great-aunt of being spoiled and selfish. Had Azalea hurt *him* in some way and he'd always held onto that? Or was there something more that Zaylie was missing?

Whatever the answer, she could see why Gran had never liked him.

Shifting uncomfortably in her seat, she asked, "Is there a particular person you can think of that she hurt?"

Mr. Beecher blew out a puff of smoke before saying nonchalantly, "Not that I can recall."

Feeling rather annoyed, Zaylie frowned and asked, "Then how can you accuse her of such things?"

Snatching the cigar from his mouth, Mr. Beecher leaned forward and hissed, "Because I *knew* her, young lady, and I know what she was capable of. She used her good looks to get what she wanted, and I knew it would backfire on her someday. She didn't love that Russell fellow; she was just using him."

"Using him for what, Mr. Beecher?" Zaylie asked, raising an eyebrow.

Making an obvious attempt to bring himself back under control, Mr. Beecher leaned his stiff body back against the sofa and crossed his bony legs.

"For whatever she could get out of him," he replied with a shrug.

"And you think she got what she wanted and then killed him?" she pressed.

With a small smirk, Mr. Beecher stated, "Apparently so."

Zaylie glanced over at Ryker, who was watching her with a look that said, "Now I know why your grandmother hates this guy."

"So, you think she stole those diamonds?" Zaylie asked.

Mr. Beecher took another long puff on his cigar before answering. "I'd say let the facts speak for themselves," he replied smoothly. "She was the only person found at the crime scene. Her fingerprints were on the safe, and she was murdered a few weeks later. It all seems very obvious to me that she had a partner who ended up turning on her. Who knows? Maybe Russell was also involved and they killed him, too."

"If what you say is true, then wouldn't the partner have ended up with the diamonds instead of Azalea?" Zaylie wanted to know.

Glancing at his watch, Mr. Beecher said, "I'm sorry, but I have another meeting in fifteen minutes." He stood to his feet and motioned toward the door. "I'm afraid you'll have to leave now."

"Thank you for your time, Mr. Beecher," Zaylie said, trying to hide her irritation. "In case I think of more questions, would it be okay if I stopped by again sometime?"

Dale's silver eyes glinted as he replied coolly, "No, I don't think so. Good day."

With that, he turned and left the room, leaving Zaylie and Ryker to stare after him in silence. Spinning on her heel, Zaylie marched toward the door with a huff.

"What a rude old man," she muttered under her

breath. Glancing around the fancy penthouse once more, she asked Ryker in a low voice, "What did Gran say he used to do for a living? His suit alone would have cost a fortune."

"I don't think anyone really knows how he made his money," Ryker replied. "From what I've heard, he's always been very vague about it. Maybe he inherited a good bit from the sale of the bank?"

"He would have had to split that between Brenda and my grandfather Joseph," Zaylie replied. "I can't think that was enough to support this kind of lifestyle all these years."

As they left the apartment and closed the door behind them, Zaylie announced that she would be taking the stairs.

"Afraid to be alone with me again?" Ryker asked with a wink.

Giving him a look, Zaylie raised an eyebrow and asked, "Don't you think I should be after the way you acted?"

His eyes widening innocently, Ryker asked, "What do you mean? I was only trying to distract you from having a panic attack."

"Well, that's beside the point anyway," she stated. "I don't think I'll ever get into another elevator again after that horrific experience."

As she marched toward the staircase, she could hear the laughter in Ryker's voice as he called out, "That's an excuse and you know it, Zaylie Layne. Just admit it; you're afraid to be that close to me again."

Zaylie rounded the corner, not bothering to answer him as she looked for the stairs. Perhaps what he said was true, but she wasn't about to admit it, especially to him. Had he really simply been trying to distract her? Or was he planning to kiss her? She might never know, but as she thought about that dark elevator and the feel of Ryker's fingers grazing her arm, she felt her skin flush.

Jerking the stairway door open, she stomped down the stairs in irritation. Ryker Steele, the man who annoyed her like no other and who also happened to be dating someone else, was not going to get the better of her like this. Yes, he was charming and good-looking, but he was a hopeless flirt, and she had no intention of letting him toy with her emotions. He'd simply caught her in a weak and vulnerable moment, and that was that.

It wouldn't happen again.

Dale Beecher listened at the door as the two young people left his apartment. He didn't really have another appointment in fifteen minutes; he'd simply wanted to get rid of them. He hadn't cared for that Layne girl's attitude; not only did she look like Azalea, but she was pushy like her, too. He didn't like pushy, opinionated women; he never had.

Walking into the bedroom where he could have total privacy, he pulled out his cell phone and made a call. This situation with Azalea's body being found, the questions being asked, and the rumors being spread was getting out of hand. He was growing tired of hearing about Azalea Layne. She'd always managed to be the center of attention, and she was still doing it over fifty years later.

CHAPTER 20

Azalea - 1966

Attending Papa's funeral only days after Russell's made me wonder if I was simply having a nightmare instead of living in reality. As I watched that lonely, wooden casket being lowered into the ground and covered over with dirt, it was almost more than I could bear. Mama cried the entire time, and even though it was expected to have everyone over to the house afterward, I knew she wasn't up to it. If it caused more gossip and scandal, so be it. I just didn't care anymore.

Joseph held Mama up as we walked into the house after the funeral was over. Annemarie and Aunt Maggie walked with me, both grave and silent. I felt hurt and angry and so very tired, but I couldn't rest. Not until I knew what my father had discovered the day he died.

"I'll help Joseph put Mother to bed," Annemarie said softly as she hurried into the master bedroom.

Aunt Maggie and I went into the kitchen to fix some sweet tea, both of us lost in our own thoughts. My mother's sister lived just outside of Jacksonville, but I hadn't seen her since Christmas. She was a wealthy widow who loved to travel; she'd recently returned from spending two months in Europe.

"Azalea, I've been thinking," Maggie stated, her tone serious. When I looked up at her and raised my eyebrows questioningly, she continued, "Your mother isn't doing well at all, and I'm worried about her. We both know how...well, how delicate her nerves are, and I think she needs to get away for a while."

I handed Aunt Maggie a glass of tea and asked, "So, what are you saying?"

Maggie took a sip of the cool, sweet drink before answering. "I'd like to take her home with me when I leave on Friday," she replied. "Staying here in this house with all the memories and pain is tearing her apart. You and I both can see that. I think a change of scenery will do her good."

Getting away from me and the scandal I've caused wouldn't hurt her either, I thought, knowing that Aunt Maggie was thinking the same thing.

With a nod, I said, "If she agrees to go with you, then I think it will be for the best."

Mama agreed to go home with Aunt Maggie, and telling her goodbye three days later was harder than I'd expected. Everything in my life was changing so rapidly and seeing how thin and pale Mama was scared me. As I watched them drive away, I wondered if I'd ever see her again.

Joseph asked if I'd like him and Annemarie to stay with me for a while, but I declined. I wanted the time alone to investigate everything that had happened with no interference.

The day Mama left, I went down to the bank. Cookie and Big Hal seemed surprised to see me and both gave me a warm hug. Being hugged by Big Hal felt like being enveloped by a giant bear, but I never complained.

"Honey, you should be at home," Cookie said. "You've been through so much this week."

"I needed to get out of the house," I replied. "I was hoping to speak with Papa's secretary, but I didn't see her when I came in."

Cookie and Big Hal shared a look that I couldn't quite decipher, and then Cookie said, "Mrs. Green decided to retire now that your father is…gone. Yesterday was her last day."

I was shocked. Mrs. Green had worked at the bank from the first day it opened. I understood that it would be hard to continue without Papa, but she'd always talked about how she loved her job. Had she made the decision all on her own, or was she forced into early retirement? I couldn't imagine why Cookie and Big Hal wouldn't want her around anymore, though, as they'd always spoken so highly of her abilities.

"That is quite the surprise," I stated. "She always loved working here."

"Well, things just aren't the same anymore," Cookie replied.

"We've actually been talking about selling the bank," Big Hal spoke up. "With everything that's happened, James and I aren't sure we want to continue without your father."

My eyes widened. "You're not going to pass on the legacy to your children?" I wanted to know. "Papa said that was always the dream from the start; to pass on something you all had worked so hard for."

Cookie nodded. "It was, but Brenda certainly has no interest in the bank," he replied.

"Neither does Dale," Big Hal added.

And neither does my brother, Joseph, I thought. *It seems that no one cares about what I want. Or maybe they just assume that I'll be in prison anyway and it doesn't matter.*

Looking at both men with a serious gaze, I asked, "Do either of you believe I stole those diamonds?"

Cookie guffawed and shook his head. "No, of course not!"

Big Hal never answered; he simply stood there in silence while Cookie continued to talk.

As the two men walked me out to my car a few moments later, they promised to let me know what they decided about the bank. I waved goodbye and drove straight to Mrs. Green's house.

"Why, Azalea, how good it is to see you!" the older lady gushed when she opened the door and saw me.

"It's good to see you, too," I said as she led me into the parlor.

We sat on the sofa and she reached over to pat me gently on the knee. "How are you, dear?" she asked.

"I'm okay," I replied with a brave smile. "How about you? I was so surprised when I heard you'd retired."

Mrs. Green shifted uncomfortably and glanced away. "Yes, well, I'd been there so long, and with your father gone, it just didn't feel right for me to stay."

I felt there was more to it than that, but I didn't press the issue. Instead, I pulled out Papa's pocket planner and asked, "Mrs. Green, do you have any idea who "A" was? Papa apparently went to see them the day he was killed."

Studying the note written on the planner with a furrowed brow, Mrs. Green shook her head and said, "No, honey, I'm afraid I don't. I remember your father saying he was going to be gone longer than normal for his break, but he didn't say where he was going."

With a sigh, I thanked Mrs. Green and left. As I drove toward home, I passed the fire station and stopped on a whim. As I walked inside, searching for Toby, a few of the men whistled at me. I smiled and batted my eyes at them before spotting Toby leaning over the open hood of a firetruck.

"So, you're a firefighter *and* a mechanic?" I asked, walking toward him.

Looking down at me, Toby said with a smile, "*And* a plumber; don't forget that one."

I leaned against the truck's bumper and crossed my arms. "Is that what you really want, though,

Toby? To become a plumber, like your father?"

Toby leaned back and rested an elbow against the hood. "What's wrong with that?" he wanted to know. "I sort of like the thought of carrying on family traditions."

I sighed and shook my head. "It just seems a little boring to me," I replied, shrugging. "Don't you ever find yourself wishing for...I don't know...something different? Something more exciting?"

Toby chuckled. "You always were a bit of a rebel, weren't you, Azalea?"

"I suppose," I muttered.

Climbing down from the truck, Toby eyed me for a moment as he wiped his hands on a rag. "Are you okay, Azalea?" he asked. "How are you holding up?"

Reaching up to wipe a grease smear off his cheek, I said, "Mama left today, so I'm feeling a little lost, I guess. All I've wanted the last couple of years was to leave home and live freely, but it seems like life had different plans for me. Now I wonder if I'll ever get out of that house."

Unless I go to prison, I thought, but didn't voice those words.

"Why don't you go stay with Louella for a few days?" Toby asked.

One corner of my mouth twitched upward as I gave him a side-eyed look and quipped, "That would give you a good excuse to stop by her house, wouldn't it? You could say you were coming by to see how I was doing."

Toby looked away, but not before I caught a look

of irritation on his face. "She's getting married, Azalea, so let it be," he stated in a hard tone.

"Why don't you just tell her how you feel?" I asked.

Toby looked at me then, and I saw sadness in the depths of his blue eyes. "It wouldn't matter if I did," he told me. "She loves **him,** not me, and I'm not going to ruin our friendship by making a fool of myself."

I knew he was right, but the fact that he wouldn't even try to fight for what he wanted made me angry. Pushing off the bumper, I snapped, "You're a coward, Toby," before stalking away.

As I climbed into my car and drove home, I regretted what I'd said, but I didn't go back to apologize. I'd never been good at saying "I'm sorry", and this time was no exception.

CHAPTER 21

Zaylie

When Zaylie finished reading the last sentence on that day's page, she looked up to see a troubled expression on Gran's face.

"I never suspected," she mumbled.

"That Mr. Garner was in love with you?" Zaylie gently asked as she closed the diary and placed it in her lap.

Gran looked up and nodded. "Yes," she replied softly. "Looking back now, I guess it should have been obvious, but I just never paid attention."

Tilting her head to the side, Zaylie asked, "Would it have made a difference if you'd known?"

Gran immediately shook her head. "No," she replied with a small smile. "I still would have chosen your grandfather."

Glancing at the clock on the mantle, Zaylie was shocked to find it was almost midnight. "I guess we got so caught up in Azalea's story that we lost track of time," she said as she stood up and stretched.

After they said good night and headed to their rooms, Gran stopped at her door and said in a thoughtful voice, "You know, Azalea *was* a bit of a rebel, but I never realized how restless she was. I'm starting to wonder...oh, never mind."

"You're starting to wonder if you knew her as well as you thought?" Zaylie asked.

Gran looked at Zaylie in surprise. "Yes," she replied softly. "She was like a sister to me, but do you think that in my young naivete, I overlooked some flaws in her character?"

Stepping from the bottom step of the staircase, Zaylie touched Gran's arm and asked, "Gran, are you saying you think Azalea might have actually been guilty after all?"

Gran hesitated, and Zaylie could see the war within her eyes. Finally, she squared her shoulders and said indignantly, "No, certainly not. Whatever her secret struggles were, there's no way she could have been capable of stealing those diamonds and killing Russell."

With that being said, Gran kissed Zaylie on the cheek and marched into her room, closing the door behind her. Zaylie stood there for a moment, pondering over their conversation. Gran was loyal to those she loved, Zaylie knew that, but was her loyalty fruitless in this case? Zaylie couldn't be sure, but she knew she was getting mixed signals from Azalea's diary. One minute, her great aunt seemed totally normal, but then there were those few twinges here and there that made Zaylie second-guess herself. Had Azalea been completely honest in her day-to-day writings? Or was she not telling the whole truth about everything that had happened?

As Zaylie headed upstairs to bed, she couldn't help but wonder if Great Aunt Azalea had been hiding something.

The next morning, Zaylie was surprised to see Grady Young walking into the house with Ryker.

"Mr. Whitlock said to tell you we'll be back to work first thing in the morning," Grady said with a charming smile.

Zaylie nodded, and sensing her confusion, Ryker explained, "Since Grady is such a good carpenter, I asked if he could help me out today."

"Oh, I see," she replied. "Would the two of you like some coffee before you get started?"

Both men agreed, and she showed them into the kitchen where Gran sat at the table, reading the newspaper.

"I do declare, I'm on the verge of suing this newspaper," she announced, not bothering to look up.

"Why is that, Mrs. Ferguson?" Ryker asked as he helped himself to the coffee.

Gran glanced up in surprise. "Oh, dear, I didn't realize..." Clearing her throat, she pointed to the paper and said, "Well, I'm just sick and tired of people making accusations without proper evidence."

"What did Mr. Rochelle do now?" Zaylie wanted to know, as she retrieved a mug for Grady.

"He wrote that not only did Azalea steal those diamonds, but she murdered her fiancé, too. How dare that man write such lies?"

"How do you know it's a lie?" Grady spoke up, and everyone turned to look at him.

"Because my best friend wasn't capable of murder," Gran stated, raising an eyebrow at the young man as if daring him to argue.

Grady stared right back at her, his jaw clenching. "Maybe you didn't know her as well as you thought," he replied. "Sometimes we tend to overlook the flaws of those closest to us."

"Young man, I'll have you know..."

Before Gran could finish, the doorbell rang and Ryker quickly ushered Grady out of the kitchen before he could say anything else. Zaylie was surprised at the nerve of the man and wondered what he'd meant by his last statement. She also knew from their conversation the night before that Gran had her own doubts about Azalea, which was probably why she'd been so touchy with him.

"That's probably Toby and Chase at the door," Gran said. "Will you, uh, let them in, dear?"

Zaylie looked at Gran, immediately noticing the flush in her cheeks and the way she shifted uncomfortably in her chair. After reading Azalea's diary last night, Zaylie suspected she didn't want to see Toby.

Trying to hide her smile, Zaylie nodded and hurried through the house. She opened the door and stepped back as Chase and another man carried in the new toilet.

"Is Louella here?" Mr. Garner wanted to know.

"Yes, sir, she's in the kitchen," Zaylie replied.

When Toby hurried toward the kitchen with a tight, worried expression on his face, Zaylie followed. As soon as he stepped through the swinging door and Gran saw him, Zaylie thought she was going to choke to death on her scone.

"Are you going to make it, Gran?" Zaylie asked as she patted her grandmother on the back.

"Must have gone down wrong," Gran wheezed.

Zaylie forced her twitching lips into a straight, serious line as she said, "Better be more careful next time."

Taking a gulp of her coffee, Gran looked up at Toby and asked, "Did you want to talk to me about something?"

Toby nodded and sat down across from her. "Odin Carter asked me to stop by the station yesterday afternoon," he said, tapping his fingers anxiously against the tabletop. "He questioned me for a good half hour about anything I saw or heard during those days leading up to Azalea's disappearance. Louella, I plumb felt like the man was accusing *me* of being involved somehow!"

Gran's eyes widened. "I have just about had it with that man," she blustered. "Why on earth would he think such a thing?"

Toby threw both hands outward and said, "Apparently, he remembers how close the three of us were before she disappeared and you...well, you got married."

Gran's cheeks flushed red, and she glanced away. "Well, just because we were all good friends certainly doesn't mean you were involved in her murder," she said, her tone softer than before.

"Mr. Garner," Zaylie interjected, "*do* you remember anything else from that time that could be helpful?"

Gran looked up, her brow furrowing. "Anything *else*?" she asked.

Zaylie told her what Toby had said about the dent in Great-Grandfather Layne's bumper.

"He wasn't certain the wreck was an accident," she said.

Gran looked at Toby in shock. "You never told me that, Toby," she gasped.

Mr. Garner shrugged. "I was a kid, Louella," he replied in a regretful tone. "I didn't know what to do...about a lot of things." Looking up at Zaylie, he added, "I didn't tell Odin this, but after all his questioning, there *was* one thing that popped into my mind."

"What?" Gran and Zaylie asked at the same time.

Scratching his temple, he sighed and said, "The day before Azalea's supposed disappearance, she called and asked if I could come to the house. She said she had something very important to give me, but she didn't want to talk about it over the phone. I told her I couldn't come; I believe I was stuck at the house getting ready for that awful storm. Remember that, Louella? Anyway, I always assumed she wanted to tell me goodbye before she ran off, but now I wonder if it was something much more serious than that."

They all sat in silence for a moment, pondering over what Toby had said. Why had Azalea been so insistent on seeing him that day? Had she known what was coming, that she might be killed soon, and she'd wanted to give him...what? The diary, perhaps? Or maybe even the diamonds?

"I wish now I'd done things differently...in a lot of areas," Toby stated in a heavy tone.

Sensing that the two old friends may want a few moments alone to talk, Zaylie slipped quietly from the room. She was on her way upstairs to check on Smutti when she heard an odd sound coming from Gran's room. Peering around the doorframe, her eyes widened when she spotted Chase going through the drawers in Gran's side table by the bed.

"Can I help you find something?"

At the sound of Zaylie's voice, Chase slammed the drawer shut and spun around to face her. "Uh, no," he replied, clearing his throat sheepishly. "Sorry, I was looking for...for a flashlight and thought your grandmother might keep one by her bed."

"She usually does, but the batteries died and she hasn't replaced them yet," Zaylie replied, eyeing him suspiciously. She wanted to ask what he was *really* looking for, but his helper called out from the bathroom and Chase hurried away.

Zaylie stood in the doorway for a moment,

listening as the two discussed the installation process. Had Chase possibly been looking for the diary? If so, why was he so interested in getting his hands on it?

CHAPTER 22

Azalea -1966

A storm was coming; I'd sensed it before the local news made the announcement. The overcast skies, the rough and choppy waves in the ocean, and the abnormally strong breeze all told me that a hurricane was in the Atlantic somewhere.

"Florida will start seeing an impact tonight," the newscaster said on the radio. *"It's a massive, but slow-moving system. If it stays on course, it looks like it will be coming right up the coast within the next few days."*

We were accustomed to hurricanes, so everyone on the island quickly set about preparing for the strong winds and rain. Thankfully, since our house was so high on the bluff, I didn't have to worry about flooding, but many others on the island did. The wind, however, was a different story, so I called J.R. Whitlock and asked if he could come out to board up the windows. We'd gone to school together, and he'd recently started his own construction company.

"I'm slammed today and most of tomorrow," he told me over the phone. "I should be able to get started at your place late tomorrow evening."

I thanked him and hung up. Deciding to go on

to the market and stock up before everything sold out, I quickly got dressed and was just about to head into town when the telephone rang. It was Sheriff Odin Carter, and he said he needed me to come down to the station to answer a few more questions. I knew I wasn't supposed to be questioned without my lawyer, but Lloyd was busy and couldn't come to the island until well after the storm. Besides, I was curious to know what Odin wanted.

When I arrived at the station, I was immediately ushered into Odin's office. In his typical arrogant and authoritative way, he flicked a finger toward the nearest chair without saying a word. I sat and waited, eyeing him cautiously.

After shuffling through some papers on his desk, Odin retrieved one in particular and stood up. He walked around the desk until he stood before me, and with a superior look, he shoved the paper under my nose.

"Does this look familiar?" he asked, raising one eyebrow.

I took the note and carefully read it, my eyes widening slightly. It was a note I'd slipped into Russell's hand three weeks ago during the Sunday service at church. It read:

I know what we're planning is dangerous, but with you by my side, I'm not afraid of anything.

"Yes, I gave this note to Russell a few weeks ago when we were planning to elope," I replied in a cool tone as I handed the note back to Odin.

"I thought you said *he* was pressuring *you* to elope," Odin stated. He took a step back and leaned against the desk, crossing his ankles as he stared at me with a piercing gaze. "According to this note, it was the other way around."

Glancing away, I shrugged and said, "He *was* pressuring me, at first, and then I suppose I started getting excited, too."

When he didn't immediately reply, I glanced up at him. There was a smirk on his pompous face, and after a moment, he said in a victorious tone, "I have other evidence, too, that I found at Russell's house when we searched it. After this storm is over, Miss Layne, we're going to proceed with this case at full force. You're going to pay for what you did."

Standing, I raised my nose in the air and said, "I won't be coming back to this station without my lawyer." I turned on my heel then and marched from the room, head held high. Before I stepped through the door, I stopped and turned back to say haughtily, "Good luck proving anything against me, Odin."

"I don't need luck, Miss Layne," he stated, completely unruffled by my tough act. "All I need is evidence, and I have more than enough."

I didn't reply; I simply slammed the door and hurried from the station. His last words had bothered me more than I cared to admit. What supposed evidence did he have against me? Was it all just a bluff?

As I walked toward my car, I rounded the corner of the building and almost ran right into Brenda Cook and Dale Beecher. I wasn't in the mood to talk and almost groaned out loud when I realized who it was.

"I see Odin also asked you to stop by," Dale stated in a slightly annoyed tone.

Also? I hesitated, wondering what Odin wanted to see these two about.

"Uh, yes," I replied, glancing over my shoulder. "He had a couple of questions to ask me."

"Care to share?" Brenda asked, eyeing me closely.

Forcing a smile, I stepped around the two and said as I walked away, "Sorry, I don't have time to stay and chat. See y'all later!"

As I hurried toward my car, I wondered if Odin would tell Brenda and Dale about the note. Had he really found other incriminating evidence at Russell's house? If so, I felt an urgency stronger than before to get to the bottom of things.

That night, I drove out to the bank and parked one block over. The streets were eerily quiet, as everyone had headed home early to prepare their homes for the incoming storm. I crept down the road, making certain to stay among the shadows. The way the wind whistled down the road sent a chill of foreboding down my spine. Was the storm going to be worse than expected? The thought that

I might manage to slip off the island and disappear during all the confusion crossed my mind, but I pushed it away. I had to know who stole those diamonds and killed Russell. I had to clear my name.

I made it to the bank and slipped around to the back of the building. A new night guard had been hired, but he wasn't on duty yet tonight. I only hoped the security system hadn't been added to the tiny window above the back door.

When I made it to the back, I shined my flashlight around until I found a couple of old crates. I stacked them on top of each other by the back door and carefully climbed on top. I reached up to wiggle the latch on the window until it opened, and then I pulled myself through. Thankfully, I was small enough to fit, and I dropped to the floor with the stealth of a cat.

The bank was dark and quiet; the only sounds I heard were the ticking of a nearby clock and the pounding of my heart. If I got caught, Odin wouldn't hesitate to throw me back into jail, and I knew I wouldn't get out so easily this time. I wasn't sure what I would find here, if anything, but I needed to try.

Slowly, I tiptoed through the bank toward the offices. I stopped at Papa's and peered inside, my heart clenching at how barren and empty it looked. Cookie and Big Hal had already cleared it out, but I stepped inside anyway, just for a moment. I thought about all the times I'd come here throughout my life to visit Papa; I could still see him sitting at his desk, looking so strong and important. Where had those years gone? And where had Papa gone the night he died?

With a sigh, I left the room and its ghosts behind and headed to Big Hal's office. I shuffled through his desk drawers and files but came up empty. I then rummaged through the small trash can next to his desk. At the bottom of the can was a wadded-up piece of paper, which I carefully unfolded. When I held the note under the light of my flashlight, I immediately recognized Cookie's handwriting.

Reminder: We have a meeting with a potential buyer for the bank on 10/1.

–C

I stared at the note in confusion. Cookie and Big Hal said they were considering selling the bank because Papa was dead. This note, however, was written the day before the robbery. Had Papa known anything about this? If so, why hadn't he said anything? And if not, why had the two men left him out? He was just as equal of a partner as they were.

I stood up and sighed, my mind whirling. This didn't make any sense. I stuffed the note into my pocket and headed into Cookie's office, wondering if I should confront the two men with what I'd discovered. Would they know I'd broken into the bank and found the note? If so, they would probably have me arrested.

As soon as I entered Cookie's room, the first thing I noticed was the box sitting in the corner with the words "LAYNE PERSONAL" written on the side in black marker. Wondering why Cookie hadn't given the box to us, I kneeled down and carefully opened it. Inside were Papa's personal effects, including a stash of fountain pens, a couple of notebooks, and various trinkets he'd always kept sitting on his desk. I pulled out one of the notebooks and ruffled through it, my eyes filling with tears at Papa's familiar, scratchy penmanship. Something on the second to the last page caught my eye, and I stopped to read it more carefully.

Talk to A about the plane ticket.

There it was again; a mention of the mysterious "A". This time, though, Papa had said what he was talking to them about…a plane ticket. What did it mean, though? And why was this box stuffed into a corner of Cookie's office? It should have been given to Mama after Papa's funeral.

Suddenly, I heard a tapping sound, and I quickly clicked off my flashlight. I sat in the darkness, listening. Was it just the rustling of the wind I'd heard, or was someone trying to get into the bank?

Clutching the notebook in my hand, I tiptoed quietly through the bank toward the front door. I'd just made it to the front room when the rattling of the doorknob met my ears and I froze. Keeping my hand over the beam of the flashlight, I clicked it back on and pointed it toward the front door. The knob was moving. Hurrying across the room, I eased the window shade back and peered out into the darkness. A man wearing a security guard's uniform stood on the stoop with a set of keys in his hand.

Fighting panic, I turned to run from the room, hoping to make it out through the back window before the security guard came inside. Before I could make it halfway across the room, however, the lock clicked and the front door creaked open. I dove behind the counter where bank customers wrote their deposit slips, my heart pounding so rapidly that I feared the guard might hear it. The lights were flipped on as the alarm system began to beep, and I listened as the guard punched in the code, turning the system off. He then closed the door behind him and locked it, and I could hear his footsteps on the marble floor as he walked across the room toward me.

I pressed my back against the counter, and I could see the guard's shadow on the floor as he drew closer to my hiding place. He stopped on the other side of the counter, and I could hear him as he tapped his fingernails on the quartz surface. The sound echoed in my ears, matching the throbbing in my head, and I tried to think of what I was going to say when he discovered me.

Just then, the tapping stopped and the clicking of his heels sounded again as he rounded the corner of the counter. He was coming around the left side, so I slowly and quietly slid to the right, hoping I could make it around the corner before he saw me. His shiny black shoes appeared just as I pushed myself around to the opposite side. I stopped, my chest heaving as I listened. Had he seen me?

Suddenly, he began to whistle a tune, and I jerked in surprise. He then walked across the room, where he stopped to check his hair in a large, ornate mirror that hung on the wall. I peered around the corner, watching him, and when he sauntered on into the next room, I took my chance. Still clutching the notebook in one hand and the flashlight in the other, I raced across the room and, with trembling fingers, turned the lock on the door. Glancing over my shoulder one last time to make certain the guard hadn't returned and seen me, I quietly opened the door and slipped out into the night.

My shadow melted into the darkness as I raced down the street toward my car. Tree branches rustled overhead and the wind blew leaves across my path, but I never slowed my pace. Twice, I looked over my shoulder to make certain no one was following me. A thick, ominous feeling hung in the air; I could sense it down in my bones. Perhaps it was just the storm, but as I jumped into my car and quickly drove away, I continued looking in the rearview mirror until I made it home.

CHAPTER 23

Zaylie

When Saturday arrived, Zaylie got up early and met Micah at the landing to go boating. He'd texted her the night before and asked her to go with him. She was a little nervous about the outing, as she hadn't gone out with him since he broke up with her all those years ago. She told herself not to read too much into it, though. Micah just wanted to be friends, and surprisingly, she was fine with that.

It was a perfect day to be out. The sun was shining, the air was cool, and the water was calm. As Micah expertly guided the boat through the winding river channels, Zaylie sat at the bow with her face toward the sun. The wind blew softly against her skin, ruffling the tendrils around her face, and she took a deep, cleansing breath of salty air and smiled.

After a while, Micah drove out into the ocean and stopped, asking Zaylie if she'd like to fish.

"I don't have a fishing license," she replied with a frown.

Micah waved a hand in the air and shoved a fishing pole into her hands. "Oh, there's no one around to notice," he told her. With a wink, he added, "I won't tell if you won't."

Laughing, Zaylie cast her line into the water, her eyes drifting upward as she watched a pelican fly gracefully above. After a moment, her eyes drifted over to Micah, and she couldn't help but notice how handsome he looked. He'd let his curly brown hair grow out a little, and she watched as the breeze ruffled through the curls, giving him a slightly boyish look. He wore a white and navy polo with navy pants, and when he glanced her way and smiled, she caught her breath. She'd always loved his clear blue eyes, and in the sunlight, they were even more striking.

"So, the Layne family is quite the talk of the town these days," Micah commented after a few moments.

Wrinkling her nose at him, Zaylie stated drolly, "Don't remind me."

With a chuckle, Micah asked, "What do you make of all the rumors flying around? Do you believe your great aunt truly was the culprit?"

Zaylie hesitated, uncertain of how to answer. After a moment, she said, "I'm sure you've already heard, but Gran and I found Azalea's diary. I can't quite figure it out, Micah. Or, at least, I can't figure *her* out."

"What do you mean?"

Zaylie sighed. "One minute, I'm convinced she was innocent, but then..." Pausing, she tilted her head to the side as she said slowly, "But then other times...I'm not so sure. I think there may have been a side to her that Gran never saw, or maybe she just didn't **want** to see."

Just then, Zaylie's fishing line pulled taunt, and she squealed with delight. Micah hurried up behind her and, putting his arms around her waist, helped reel in one of the smallest fish Zaylie had ever caught.

"Whoa, it's a whale!" he teased. "Too bad we can't keep it."

"Hey, at least I caught something, unlike certain others on this boat," she retorted with a grin.

Micah wagged a finger in her face and said, "Just give me time, Miss Layne."

The two continued to talk and laugh as they fished, and Zaylie was reminded of the days when they were young. She'd fallen in love with him when she was just a child, and she remembered all the summer days they'd spent out on the water, just like they were now. What had happened to those two young kids? They'd been so in love...or, at least, she'd thought they were.

After a while, they decided they were hungry and put the fishing poles away. Zaylie had packed a picnic lunch for them, and they quickly devoured the delicious potato salad, ham sandwiches, sweet pickles, and brownies.

"Wow, we've really drifted a long way," Zaylie commented as Micah put the dirty bowls back into the picnic basket. Shielding her eyes from the sun, she pointed to the edge of the island and added, "Isn't that Cameron Sterling's property?"

Looking up, Micah nodded and said, "Yeah, I

didn't realize we'd come so far."

While Micah headed back to the helm, Zaylie dug through her bag for some more sunscreen. She'd never been prone to many freckles, but with her auburn hair and ivory skin, she didn't want to take any chances.

"Uh oh," she heard Micah murmur.

Turning, she saw the frown on his face and asked what was wrong.

"The motor won't start," he replied. He continued to try, but nothing happened. After a moment, he sighed and said, "I guess I'd better call in for a tow. I'm sorry, Zaylie. I certainly didn't expect our date to go like this."

Date? Zaylie blinked. While Micah called a towing company, Zaylie turned around and tried to gather her thoughts. Had he meant for this to be a date, or was that simply a slip on words?

"Well, the towing company is closed today," Micah said, interrupting Zaylie's thoughts. "Their voicemail says they're out sick."

"Can you call the coast guard?" Zaylie asked.

"They normally won't come unless it's an emergency, but I can give it a try," Micah replied.

"Wait, let me call Ryker first," Zaylie said as she grabbed her phone. "His dad has a boat; they can probably give us a tow."

When she got Ryker on the phone, he asked, "Zaylie, what are y'all doing out on the water today? We're supposed to get terrible thunderstorms this afternoon."

"Really?" she asked in surprise as she looked up at the sky. "It's clear and sunny right now."

"You know how quickly that can change around here," he replied. "I'll get Dad's boat and try to pick y'all up before the storm hits."

While they waited, Zaylie and Micah discussed the training center. It had been Micah who suggested she open a new one on the island, and she was excited to get it going.

"I get up early every morning and help my manager, Leslie, with the bookwork and anything else that's online," she said. "I'm ready to get back to doing the hands-on stuff, though. I miss working with the dogs."

Micah smiled admiringly at her. "We always had that in common, you know," he stated.

"Our love for animals?" she asked. When he nodded, she smiled and replied, "Yes, we did."

Reaching out, Micah took Zaylie's hand and said warmly, "We had more than that in common, though, didn't we?"

Zaylie felt her breath catch. There was something in his piercing gaze that made her heart pick up speed, but before she could process her thoughts, a rumble of thunder met her ears. They both turned to find that the sky was quickly becoming dark and stormy. The wind had picked up, as well, and the water was hitting against the sides of the boat with more force than before.

"Where is Ryker?" Zaylie muttered, glancing at her watch. Nearly forty minutes had passed since she'd called him.

Turning, Micah looked toward the land and said, "He should be here soon."

As the moments passed, the weather steadily grew worse. The storm was coming in quickly, and Zaylie tried to keep a feeling of worry at bay. She'd always been terrified of being caught in the open water during a storm, and when a streak of lightning suddenly split the sky, she gasped.

"Hey, it's okay," Micah assured her. Sliding closer, he wrapped an arm around her shoulders and squeezed gently.

The waves were getting rougher and the sky was growing darker by the second. Zaylie and Micah both put on lifejackets and when the rain started, they scurried to get underneath the canopy. They sat huddled against each other as the rain steadily grew stronger, beating loudly against the canopy and splashing over onto their skin and clothes.

Suddenly, a mighty clap of thunder shook the boat just as a flash of lightning lit the sky. Zaylie squeezed her eyes shut and began to pray for help to arrive soon. The boat rocked back and forth like a child's toy on a raging sea, and she clung to Micah like a lifeline.

Just then, a large wave struck the vessel and splashed over the sides, soaking them both. Zaylie hadn't thought about it until then, but Micah's boat wasn't very large and probably wasn't made for being out on the open ocean. Would it be split in two by the violence of the waves? She glanced wildly about, wondering why it was taking Ryker so long.

"It's going to be okay, Zaylie," Micah yelled over the noise of the storm. "I promise I won't let anything happen to you."

Before Zaylie could respond, a massive wave rose up out of the ocean like an angry sea monster and grabbed the tiny boat, flinging it onto its side like a rag-doll. With a scream, Zaylie slammed against Micah and they were both thrown overboard.

CHAPTER 24

Zaylie

Cold water rushed over Zaylie's body, and she gasped. She felt something catch her life jacket and roughly jerk her backward, slamming her into the boat. Twisting around, she realized it was the canopy pole; it had somehow lodged itself into the back of her jacket and wouldn't let go. As the boat rocked wildly back and forth, the pole dug painfully into her spine over and over. That was the least of her worries, though, as the boat kept pushing her beneath the surface with the rise and fall of each wave. She knew if the boat completely capsized, it would drag her under. She tried to unsnap her life jacket, but the buckles had somehow gotten twisted and she couldn't grasp them hard enough with the waves jerking her about so forcefully.

"Zaylie!" she heard Micah cry out, and she turned to see him swimming toward her.

"I-I can't get loose," she stammered, choking on water as the boat dunked her under once more.

Through the violence of the storm, Zaylie could feel Micah's touch as he swam up beside her and tried to get her loose from the pole. The waves and boat bounced them through the water like a pinball. Suddenly, the boat let out a loud moan and flipped completely over, pushing them both beneath the surface.

Zaylie felt panic shoot through her body like the pricks of a million needles. She fought against the water that engulfed her like a black cloud. She could no longer feel Micah beside her. Had the boat knocked him out? Was he drowning? They were both going to die; she could feel it in her bones.

Suddenly, a strong hand pierced through the water and grabbed her life jacket. She couldn't see, but she could feel the buckles twisting as Micah tried to get them loose. After what felt like an eternity, they finally snapped open and she was free. Micah grabbed her by the hand and pulled her from beneath the boat, where he pushed her forcefully toward the surface. She broke through the water and gasped in as much air as she could before going back down again. She was exhausted, and without her life jacket, she could barely stay afloat in the raging sea, but she continued to try.

Everything was spinning wildly out of control as Zaylie pushed her head above the water and looked around. She tried to call out for Micah, but she could barely force out the words. Where was he? Had the water sucked him back under?

Just then, through the blinding rain, she spotted a boat. It was racing toward them, and she thought she heard Ryker's voice. She waved a hand in the air, trying desperately to stay above the water. She was a good swimmer, but her legs were beginning to cramp and the waves were just too strong.

Oh, God, where is Micah? she cried on the inside.

Tears streamed down her face, melting into the salty sea. What if he was dead? He'd been under the water for what seemed like hours; he couldn't last much longer.

Suddenly, Micah's head broke through the surface of the water only a few feet from the boat. Ryker's dad was driving, and he quickly steered the boat in that direction. They hadn't spotted her yet, but she could see Ryker leaning out over the side of the boat, looking for her.

"Zaylie!" she heard him cry.

With every ounce of strength she had left, Zaylie opened her mouth and screamed at the top of her lungs. At the exact moment, a clap of thunder erupted from the sky. Had he heard her? She didn't think she could force herself to cry out again. Her body ached and trembled, and she could feel the strength of the ocean pulling her down. It was as if it had her within its mighty grip and she couldn't get free.

The world around her was starting to fade. Just before Zaylie sank beneath the surface, she saw Ryker dive into the water, but it was no use. It was too late; he'd never be able to get to her in time.

Zaylie's body was numb as she floated down into the ocean's depths. Oddly enough, everything seemed quiet and peaceful down below. She told herself to fight, to try to swim upward just one more time, but her limbs seemed frozen and unable to move. Stars floated before her eyes, and when her lungs began to scream in pain, she opened her mouth to inhale the salty ocean.

Suddenly, two hands grabbed her by the arms and jerked her upward. Zaylie's eyes bulged open as she snapped out of the stupor that had come over her. With a gasp, she choked and gagged as water filled her mouth and nose. With panic once again setting in, she began to fight, but the hands that held her were strong enough to withstand the flailing of her arms and legs.

When they finally reached the surface, Zaylie was shaking so badly that she feared she was having convulsions. She scrambled to grab onto the strong shoulders that held her up, gasping for air as the water she'd swallowed spewed from her stomach. The storm still raged all around, but all Zaylie could hear was the pounding of her heart.

"It's okay," a gentle voice said next to her ear. "You're okay."

Leaning back, Zaylie looked at Ryker through hazy, blurry eyes. She wanted to ask about Micah, but she was just too exhausted to form the words.

With one arm wrapped firmly around her waist, Ryker swam toward the boat that was quickly heading their way. The waves continued to beat against them, but Ryker acted as though pushing himself through the stormy ocean with only one arm while holding Zaylie with the other was no effort at all.

Seconds later, the boat was at their side and Zaylie was being hoisted onto its deck. Mr. Steele, Ryker's dad, helped her sit down beneath the large canopy and then wrapped her in a beach towel.

"Oh, Zaylie, thank God you're alright."

Zaylie turned to see Micah kneeling down beside her, his face filled with both relief and torment. She wound her arms around his neck and began to cry.

"I'm so glad you're safe," she whispered.

Micah wrapped his arms around her waist and buried his face in her hair. They sat in that embrace for a moment while Mr. Steele turned the boat and headed home. When Micah finally released her to take his seat as they bounced along the waves, Zaylie turned to see Ryker sitting out in the rain, watching them. There was a look on his face that she couldn't quite discern, but it was akin to anger.

When they finally reached the shore, the rain had stopped and the storm was over. Micah was a bit unsteady on his feet, so Mr. Steele helped him climb from the boat while Ryker assisted Zaylie. He jumped down first and then reached back up for her. After swinging her down from the boat, he kept his hands wrapped firmly around her waist and pulled her closer against his chest.

"Hey," he said, and when she looked up at him, he continued, "Don't ever scare me like that again. Okay?"

"I hope that *I'm* never scared like that again," she replied in a hoarse voice. "Thank you, Ryker. You saved my life."

He stared down at her for a moment, his eyes

filled with a war of emotions. She'd never seen him like this before; his devil-may-care attitude had been replaced with worry and concern...and something else. She'd never seen him this serious.

"Y'all coming?"

At his father's question, Ryker released her and stepped back but kept a hand at her elbow as they walked up the dock. When they joined Micah and Mr. Steele on the landing, Ryker said he would drive Zaylie home.

"I can drive," she insisted.

"You can barely walk," Ryker retorted. "I'll drive you home and Dad can pick me up at your house."

"I can take her home..." Micah attempted to say.

"I think you've done enough today, Pierce," Ryker interrupted, his jaw clenching.

Micah looked at Ryker in surprise. "What is that supposed to mean?" he demanded.

Turning a steely gaze on the veterinarian, Ryker stated, "Maybe next time you should check the weather before you take someone out on the water."

"I did," Micah shot back. "I had planned for us to be back before it hit, but then the motor died and we were stranded."

"You should never have left the river in the first place," Ryker replied, his eyes flashing. "Your boat was too small."

"Look, I don't know why you're attacking me like this, but..."

Ryker stepped forward, his face filled with such

anger that Zaylie was afraid he was going to hit Micah. She opened her mouth to intervene but stopped when Mr. Steele gave her a look and shook his head.

"She could have died, Pierce," Ryker ground out in a harsh tone. "Do you not understand that? She wasn't even wearing a life jacket! She would have died if Dad and I hadn't gotten there just in the nick of time."

"Ryker, please..." Zaylie said softly.

Both men glared at each other in silence until Micah finally turned and walked away. Zaylie wanted to cry as she watched him climb into his truck and drive out of the parking lot, but she managed to hold herself together. How on earth had everything gone so badly? She felt terrible about the whole thing.

Mr. Steele cleared his throat and Ryker turned back to look at them. His face no longer held any anger, but he was still clearly very upset.

"Are you ready to go?" he asked Zaylie.

She nodded, and just before they turned to walk to his truck, she thanked Mr. Steele for his help.

The drive home was quiet and tense. Having such a close brush with death had left Zaylie shaken in more ways than one, and all she wanted was to get home to Gran and Smutti.

Looking over at Ryker, she noticed that his jaw was still clenched and his shoulders were stiff and rigid. With a sigh, she said softly, "Micah saved my life, too, you know. When the boat capsized, the canopy pole caught my life jacket and dragged me under. If he hadn't dived beneath the water and unbuckled my jacket, I would have drowned."

Ryker didn't say anything at first, but she noticed that his grip on the steering wheel loosened a bit. After a moment, he looked at her and said, "I'm thankful for that, but what he did was still irresponsible. He should never have taken that boat out onto the ocean, especially with a storm coming in."

Zaylie didn't respond; she knew he was right. Still, she felt bad for Micah because she knew what he'd done was not intentional.

As they drove past the gate at Azalea Bluff, she asked, "How on earth did you manage to swim through those waves and find me beneath the water?"

Zaylie saw the old Ryker starting to return when a grin slowly spread across his face. With twinkling eyes, he said, "I've done more intense missions than that, Miss Layne, or have you forgotten I was a SEAL?"

Laughing, Zaylie shook her head and shot back, "How could I when you remind me every chance you get?"

"Just make sure you don't forget." He winked.

When they pulled up in front of the house and parked, Zaylie surprised them both by leaning across the console and planting a kiss on Ryker's cheek.

"Thank you again," she said. "You were right;

if you hadn't gotten there in the nick of time, I would have died. And," she added teasingly as she sat back and unbuckled her seatbelt, "if you didn't have that special COOP training."

Ryker smiled warmly at her. "It was my pleasure," he said. Tapping his chin, he added, "You know, it seems like I keep saving your life. I guess you should keep me around, huh?"

"Or stop getting into so much trouble," she quipped as she climbed from the car.

Zaylie waited until Ryker could help her up the front porch steps, as her legs were still very weak. As soon as they walked inside and Gran found out what happened, she nearly went through the roof. Smutti also seemed to sense something was wrong, as she stayed glued to her master's side with a worried look in her golden eyes. When Gran insisted that Zaylie go to the hospital, Zaylie refused.

"Okay, fine, if you're going to be stubborn, then go change out of those wet clothes and I'll fix you some hot broth," Gran demanded.

Ryker helped Zaylie up the stairs, and when they reached her bedroom, she said, "I think I've got it from here."

Wiggling his eyebrows, he asked, "You sure?"

Zaylie laughed. "Yes, Mr. Steele, I'm sure. Now go home; I think I just heard your dad pull up."

Reaching up, Ryker touched her on the chin, his gaze warm. They were standing so close that their arms were touching, and Zaylie felt a flush rush over her body. When Ryker stepped back, said goodbye, and walked away, she took a deep breath and shook herself.

It's been a long day, she told herself as she stepped into her bedroom and shut the door. *Don't get any silly ideas.*

After taking a quick shower and changing into a warm pair of pajamas, Zaylie collapsed into bed with Smutti at her side and instantly fell asleep.

CHAPTER 25

Azalea - 1966

The next morning, I went over to Louella's house to help her and her ailing mother pack up a few of their things. They were planning to stay with Lou's fiancé and his family until the storm blew over; I hoped their poor little house would even still be standing after it was all over.

"Where's your mother?" I asked when I arrived at their house.

"Fergie is driving her over to his parents' house," Louella explained. "He'll be back in a little while."

"Fergie" was Lou's pet name for her fiancé, and even though I'd never said so, I found it annoying.

"Won't you come with us, Azalea?" Lou asked hopefully. "Or at least go stay with your brother? I hate to think of you staying in that big old house all alone."

"Joseph and Annemarie keep saying the same thing, but I'll be fine," I assured her.

As I grabbed a few perishable items from the refrigerator and put them into paper bags, I kept thinking about Papa's note in the notebook I'd taken from the bank last night. I'd spoken to Joseph about it this morning over the phone and he had no idea who the mysterious "A" was. When he asked where I found the notebook, I changed the subject and quickly got off the phone. As soon as I was finished here with Lou, I planned to go over to Cookie and Cynthia's to ask a few questions.

"How are you holding up, Azalea?"

At Lou's question, I blinked and looked up, not having realized she'd come back into the room. Shaking my head of its jumbled thoughts, I said, "I feel like I'm going crazy. Lou, what will I do if Odin manages to send me to prison? I'll lose my mind if I have to stay locked in a cell for the rest of my life."

With a sigh, Louella said, "Azalea, you haven't done anything wrong, so I truly don't think you have anything to worry about. Once this storm is over, I believe your brother and lawyer will ramp up their efforts to clear you of all charges."

I folded down the top of one of the paper bags and placed it in a nearby box. Turning to look at my friend, I said, "I hope you're right, but if you're not, I won't go to prison, Lou. I'll run away and become a fugitive before I let that happen."

With a smile pulling at her lips, Louella said, "You always were a fighter, weren't you?" Coming over to pat my arm, she added, "I don't believe it will come to that, though."

Suddenly feeling a little emotional, tears filled my eyes and I pulled her into a hug. "Thank you for being the sister I never had," I said softly.

"Thank *you* for being my absolute dearest friend," Louella replied.

Lou pulled away then and got back to work,

but not before I saw the tears glistening in her own eyes. She'd had a hard life, and I knew that watching her mother slowly fade away was killing her. I also knew how much she loved my parents and how hard she was taking everything that had happened. I hoped it would all be over soon, but I had a feeling that things might not end the way I wanted them to.

A couple of hours later, I arrived at the Cook residence. Most of the windows were already boarded up, and I spotted J.R. Whitlock on top of a ladder as he finished with the second-story windows. I waved to him as I went inside, and he called out to say he'd be heading to my house soon.

"Hey, what are you doing here?" Brenda asked in surprise when she saw me.

"I brought over some stuff I thought y'all might need for the storm," I replied, nodding at the box I was carrying. "There are some flashlights, candles, and canned goods."

"That was nice of you," Brenda said with a smile. Walking toward me, she held out her hands and added, "Here, I'll take the box."

Handing over my load, I glanced around and asked, "Is your dad here?"

"He's upstairs, helping J.R. with the windows," Brenda replied. Eyeing me curiously, she asked, "Did you need to see him about something?"

I hesitated, trying to maintain a neutral

expression on my face. "I just needed to ask him a quick question," I replied, smiling.

I could tell Brenda wanted to ask me what it was about, but she simply waved a hand toward the staircase and told me to go on up. When I arrived on the second floor, I found Cookie in one of the spare bedrooms. Their maid, Astrid, was standing beside him, handing him nails as he and J.R. covered the window.

"Hi, Astrid," I greeted the pretty young woman with a smile.

Upon hearing my voice, Cookie turned to see me, a look of surprise crossing his face. "Azalea, honey, is everything okay?" he asked.

Glancing uncertainly at Astrid, I said, "I was hoping I could speak with you about something? It won't take long."

Cookie nodded and said, "Certainly. J.R. is moving over to the next room, Astrid. Would you mind helping him for a moment?"

Once Astrid was gone, I said, "Odin seems to think he has found some incriminating evidence, and once the storm is over, he's planning to put me in prison."

Cookie's eyes widened. "We're not going to let that happen, honey."

Eyeing him closely, I pulled Papa's notebook from my purse and said, "I'm not planning to let it happen either. In fact, I plan to do whatever I can to prove my innocence. Cookie, why did you have a box full of Papa's things in your office?"

Cookie blinked in surprise. Glancing at the notebook I held, his gaze narrowed slightly, and he asked, "How did you know about that box?"

"Oh, you know me," I said flippantly. "I have a way of getting my hands on whatever I want. Cookie, why did you and Big Hal lie to me?"

Raising his eyes to meet mine, Cookie asked, "What are you talking about?"

"You both told me that you'd decided to sell the bank *after* Papa died, but I discovered that y'all met with a potential buyer *before* his death," I replied.

Cookie sighed. "Azalea, there's a lot you don't understand. You should just let Big Hal and me handle..."

"I plan to tell Odin all of this," I interrupted. "There are some suspicious notes here in Papa's notebook that hopefully he can help me figure out."

Cookie stared at me in shock. "Azalea, it almost sounds like you're accusing *us* of something," he said. "Of what, though, I'm not certain. Do you think we stole those diamonds, killed Russell, and...what? Your father, too? Azalea, his death was an accident. Why are you doing this?"

His tone was filled with hurt, but I pushed away the feeling of guilt. I wasn't going to prison, and I had to do whatever it took to prove my innocence.

"All I'm saying is that there's more here than meets the eye," I replied, shrugging. "I'm sorry, Cookie. I'm not trying to hurt you."

I turned then and walked away, trying to ignore the tremor in my hands as I opened the door and stepped out into the hall. Cynthia was standing there, and by the hard look on her face, I knew she'd been listening to our conversation. I nodded to her and continued down the stairs without a word. I thought about going to Big Hal's next but wasn't sure if I should. Was I killing off every connection I had in this world? These people were my family; maybe not by blood, but they were still a part of my life and I was hurting them.

"You should stay with us through the storm, Azzy," Brenda called out from the parlor as I passed by.

I stopped and turned toward her. There was something in her voice that made me hesitate; it was almost as if she were patronizing me. When I looked at her, though, there was nothing but innocence on her face, and I wondered what else I was misjudging.

"Thanks, but I'll be fine," I told her with a smile.

As I walked out to my car, I felt pricks of shame gnawing at my conscience. Was I doing the wrong thing by trying to throw the guilt on someone else?

No, I told myself as I drove away. *Someone has to pay for all of this, and it's not going to be me.*

CHAPTER 26

Zaylie

Z aylie couldn't stay awake to continue reading any more of the diary, so with a yawn, she closed the book.

"Is that why you were so convinced she'd run away?" Zaylie asked. "Because she told you she would rather become a fugitive than be sent to prison?"

Gran nodded. "Yes," she replied. "I never dreamed she'd been killed."

"Did you know it annoyed her that you called Gramp 'Fergie'?" Zaylie asked with a laugh.

Gran pursed her lips in annoyance. "No, I did not," she stated. "I'm surprised she never told me. She was very outspoken, you know."

With another yawn, Zaylie asked, "Do you think Cookie or Big Hal had something to do with everything that happened?"

Gran sighed and shook her head. "I don't know, Zaylie," she replied in a heavy tone. "I find it hard to believe; they were both such nice men."

After Gran rubbed some medicine on the cuts on Zaylie's back, Zaylie kissed her good night and climbed up to bed with Smutti pattering softly along beside her. Zaylie's phone chimed, and she quickly tapped the screen, expecting the text to be from Micah. It was from Rita instead, and she frowned slightly. She'd expected Micah to text and check on her, but he hadn't. She hoped he was okay.

After spending the next five minutes convincing her best friend that she wasn't going to die in her sleep, Zaylie turned her phone off and went to bed. She expected to fall right to sleep, but as soon as her head hit the pillow, her mind started racing. Flashes of lightning in the sky and angry waves in the ocean as they swept over her and pulled her under filled her thoughts. She tossed and turned and tried to think of something else, but every time she closed her eyes, her mind went back to the traumatic events of the day. She also wondered if her nap that afternoon was keeping her from sleeping.

Finally, she sat up in bed and grabbed her phone. As she scrolled through social media, a familiar face popped onto the screen and she paused, her brow furrowing. It was a friend-suggestion for Shawn Eaton, their property caretaker. In his profile picture, he was standing next to Dale Beecher. Zaylie clicked on the picture, and her eyes widened in surprise at the caption.

"Happy Grandparent's Day," it read. *"Though life has taken us in different directions, you'll always be my grandfather and I'll always love you."*

Zaylie stared at the photo in shock. Shawn was Dale's grandson? How had she never known that? She quickly took a screenshot of the picture and texted it to Rita, asking her about the situation.

"You didn't know they were related?" Rita asked. When Zaylie said no, she replied, *"Old Mr. Beecher disowned his daughter when she married a man he didn't approve of. From what Shawn has told me, he tried to reconcile things several years ago. Mr. Beecher didn't approve of Shawn's career choice, though, so the old tyrant cut him off again."*

"How did I not know about this?" Zaylie wanted to know. *"The man works for us, for goodness' sake."*

"He rarely talks about it," Rita replied. *"Honestly, in a way, I think he hates the old man. He tries to act like he doesn't, but there's a lot of resentment there."*

Zaylie couldn't believe Gran had never mentioned this to her before, but she planned to ask her about it first thing in the morning.

When the morning came, Zaylie felt like she'd been run over by a log truck. She hobbled into the bathroom, and after taking a long hot shower, she slowly started to feel better. After dressing for church and quickly pulling her hair into a half-up-half-down style, she went downstairs to join Gran for breakfast.

"How are you feeling?" Gran asked, eyeing Zaylie from the kitchen table.

"Like running a marathon," Zaylie teased as she popped a blueberry bagel into the toaster. After pouring herself a cup of coffee, she asked Gran about the situation with Shawn and Dale.

"Those two are related?" Gran asked in surprise. "I never knew that, but then I never kept up with the Beechers; they all thought they were too good for the likes of me. I do seem to remember hearing the girls at church say something several years ago about Dale disowning his daughter, but I didn't pay much attention."

"What about Brenda?" Zaylie questioned, moving on to Cookie's daughter. "Does she have any children?"

"From what I've heard, she couldn't have children," Gran replied. "But who knows? Maybe she just didn't *want* kids."

They continued to talk about Azalea and the diary until it was time to leave for church. When they arrived and walked inside, Zaylie's eyes immediately drifted toward Micah. He was standing in the foyer, looking quite handsome in a blue suit as he talked to some friends. When he saw her, he excused himself and headed her way.

"Hey, how are you feeling this morning?" he asked. There was a coolness in his tone that caught Zaylie by surprise, and when she looked into his eyes, she could see that his gaze seemed guarded.

"Sore," she replied with a half-smile, "and a little washed-out, but I'm okay. How are you?"

"Upset over everything that happened," he replied. "I hope you know that if the motor hadn't died, I would have gotten you home before that storm hit. I would never do something so irresponsible."

"Of course, I know you wouldn't ever do anything to put me in danger," Zaylie assured him.

"Apparently, Ryker didn't think so," he replied tensely. "I was afraid you were in agreement with him."

"Since when have I ever agreed with Ryker?" Zaylie asked drolly, causing Micah to chuckle. With a soft smile, she added, "He was just concerned, that's all. I told him later how you saved me from staying trapped underneath that boat. If it hadn't been for both you *and* Ryker, I would have drowned."

With a small, relieved sigh, Micah seemed to relax. "I'm just glad you're okay," he said, reaching out to touch her arm. "I was worried sick about you."

"I'm glad you're okay, too," she replied warmly.

The musicians started to play their instruments then, alerting everyone that the service was about to start. Zaylie and Micah went their separate ways, and as Zaylie hurried into the sanctuary to take her seat next to Gran, she bumped right into Ryker.

"As sore as I know you are this morning, you'd better borrow some of your grandmother's liniment," he told her teasingly.

"Hey, I'm used to over-taxing my body," she retorted. "Have you forgotten all the daring search-and-rescue missions I've been on?"

"Ah, yes, the adventurous and fearless Miss Layne. How could I have forgotten?" he replied with a smile. Glancing to one side, he nodded his head toward Micah and commented, "It seems he's in much better spirits now; you must have really buttered him up."

Zaylie frowned. "I wouldn't call it that, but yes, I did talk to him."

Ryker's eyes glinted as he leaned toward her and said in a low tone, "Come now, Zaylie, I saw the look on his face when you first started talking; he looked like a pouty little boy. By the time you finished with him, though, I expected him to walk away whistling a tune. Did he even check on you last night?"

Zaylie bristled. "He felt like I agreed with what you said about his being irresponsible, so I told him that wasn't the case," she stated. "And *you* didn't check on me either."

"I'm the one who took you home, remember? And I was with Rita when she asked how you were," he replied smoothly. "So, his poor little feelings were hurt, huh? When you told him you didn't agree with me, is that when he started to feel better?"

The cynicism in his voice made Zaylie furious, and with flashing eyes, she snapped, "You don't have to act so superior, Ryker Steele. I told him I didn't agree with you because I *don't.* Have you ever considered the fact that you might actually be wrong about some things?"

A slow, self-satisfied grin slid across Ryker's face, and he said with an annoying chuckle, "There's that fiery temper that matches your hair."

Lips pursed, Zaylie stated emphatically, "I have **auburn** hair, thank you, and I do not have a fiery temper. You just bring out the worst in me."

"It's got to be there, though, for me to bring it out," he replied with a wink before sauntering off to his seat.

Zaylie stared after him for a moment before stomping off to her own seat. The arrogance of that man never ceased to annoy the life out of her. He was one of those people who just needed to be slapped.

As Zaylie took her seat next to Gran, she noticed Grady Young sitting just across the aisle, and it appeared his mother was in town for the weekend. The woman leaned around her son to shoot a dirty look at Gran, and Zaylie frowned in confusion.

"Why is she glaring at you like that?" she whispered to Gran.

"Remember how Azalea wrote that Russell's family was convinced Azalea killed him?" Gran asked. "Apparently, the Madison family passed their opinions down to their descendants."

"You had nothing to do with it, though," Zaylie stated.

"No, but I supported Azalea, which made me the enemy," Gran said.

The pastor began to speak, and everyone's attention was quickly diverted. Throughout the service, though, Zaylie kept thinking about the hate-filled look on Grady's mother's face. Did

Grady feel the same way? If so, he most likely resented working at the Layne home, which left Zaylie with an unsettled feeling.

CHAPTER 27

Zaylie

The next morning, when the work crew arrived at Azalea Bluff, Zaylie was summoned outside to discuss a problem with the blueprints. Once that was settled, Zaylie turned to Alan Whitlock and asked if he'd gotten a chance to talk to his father.

As Alan folded the blueprints, he said, "I tried, but Dad doesn't remember much."

Zaylie tilted her head in puzzlement. "Really?" she asked. "When I was there, he seemed to remember something in particular that he overheard."

Alan shrugged. "His mind isn't what it used to be," he replied. "He was probably just confused."

"I don't think he was, Mr. Whitlock," Zaylie insisted.

Eyeing her for a moment, Alan finally sighed and said, "Okay, Miss Layne, if you want to give it another try, I can go out there with you one evening this week after work. I'll let you know when."

With a smile, Zaylie thanked him and went back inside. As soon as she stepped into the kitchen, she was surprised to find Mr. Toby sitting next to Gran at the table. His hand rested over hers, and they seemed to be having a private conversation. When he saw Zaylie, he quickly moved his hand and stood up.

"Morning, Zaylie," he greeted her with a nod. Glancing at Gran, he cleared his throat and added, "I was just about to get to work," and hurried from the kitchen.

With raised eyebrows, Zaylie looked at Gran and asked, "What was that all about?"

Gran heaved a sigh and said, "He was sharing some concerns he has about Chase."

"What kind of concerns?" Zaylie asked curiously as she joined Gran at the table.

"Well, you know what a hard life he's had," Gran replied.

"You mean how his mom ran off when he was a baby and then his dad died right after we moved to Crescent Moon?"

Gran nodded. "Toby did the best he could with him, but Chase was always wild and he finally ran off when he was eighteen. Toby didn't even know where he was until he suddenly showed back up on the island a few months ago. Toby is hoping Chase will want to take over the company, but Chase isn't acting overly interested. Plus," Gran looked around and lowered her voice as she continued, "one of their clients called Toby first thing this morning to say that an old family heirloom is missing. Toby said Chase was working in their kitchen on Friday."

Zaylie's eyes widened. "Do they think Chase stole

it?"

Gran shrugged. "They didn't accuse anyone; they just simply asked Toby if Chase remembered seeing the heirloom. Toby hasn't talked to Chase about it yet."

Zaylie sat back in her chair and shook her head. "Wow," she murmured, thinking of how she'd caught Chase digging through Gran's side table. She hadn't told Gran about the incident and wondered if perhaps she should now. Or, better yet, maybe she should just keep an extra close eye on Chase while he worked in their house.

As Zaylie got up to fix herself a cup of coffee, she said teasingly, "I thought maybe you two were talking about something a little more, you know, personal."

Gran's cheeks flushed, and she said tartly, "No, of course not. Why would you think such a thing?"

"Because I think Mr. Toby still has a thing for you," she replied.

Twisting around in her seat, Gran stated emphatically, "Listen, young lady, your grandfather was the love of my life, and I have no desire to get involved with anyone else."

Her lips twitching, Zaylie said, "Gramp may have been the love of *your* life, but I think *you* were the love of Mr. Toby's life."

With a gasp, Gran said, "Zaylie Layne, hush your mouth! Toby was married for nearly forty years; he actually got married right before I did."

"What was his wife's name?" Zaylie wanted to

know.

"Astrid."

Zaylie was pouring the cream into her coffee and hesitated, frowning. Where had she heard that name recently? Turning to look at Gran, she asked, "Wasn't that the name of James Cook's maid?"

Tilting her head, Gran thought it over for a moment. "Yes, you're right," she said. "I'd forgotten all about that."

"And they married right before you and Gramp?"

Gran nodded. Clearing her throat, she said, "They, uh, actually had Chase's father pretty quickly after they were married."

Noting the tone in her grandmother's voice, Zaylie asked, "How soon?"

"Six months."

Zaylie's eyebrows shot up. "So, he and Astrid had been dating for a while."

Gran shrugged, not quite meeting Zaylie's gaze. "I guess, but I never knew it. The first I ever heard of the two of them being together was two weeks before they went to the courthouse and were married by a justice of the peace."

Zaylie was quite surprised by this information, but before she could ask any more questions, her phone rang. Seeing that it was Rita, Zaylie quickly answered.

"Why did you ever suggest that I become a drama teacher?" Rita all but yelled into the phone. "These kids are monsters! They won't listen to a word I say. The girls won't stop talking and giggling, and the boys have destroyed the music I wrote. Zaylie, they've turned my masterpiece into spitballs and paper airplanes!"

Zaylie could picture her best friend looking completely frazzled with a pencil sticking out of her messy hair and spitballs stuck to her blouse. With a laugh, she said, "Come on, Rita, it can't be that bad."

"It's worse!" Rita screeched. "I think I may have to go back to Broadway."

Zaylie could hear the sound of laughter and chairs scraping across the floor in the background, and she asked, "Are you supposed to be making phone calls right in the middle of class?"

"Desperate times call for desperate measures," she retorted. "I wasn't meant to be a teacher, Zaylie. Do you think the theater in Atlanta will take me back?"

"Rita Steele, I'm surprised at you," Zaylie said sternly, placing a hand on her hip. "You'd give up this quickly and return to a job where your boss constantly made advances toward you? I'm sure trying to teach kids is tough, but I never thought of you as a quitter. You've barely been there a month!"

"You know what? You're right," Rita said indignantly. "Why should I be intimidated by a bunch of snotty-nosed kids? I'm the adult here, and it's time I took charge. Thank you, Zaylie." Rita blew out a breath, and Zaylie could picture her friend standing up straight and squaring her shoulders. "Okay, kids, listen up!"

The phone went dead, and Zaylie pushed it into her pocket with a chuckle. Although Gran came in at a close second, Zaylie had never known anyone quite as vivacious as her best friend. If anyone could handle those kids and teach them the true art and magic of drama class, it would be Rita.

After Gran headed to the market, Zaylie went upstairs to get Smutti. The poor dog had been cooped up too much the last few days, and Zaylie planned to take her for a long walk on the beach. The two had just come down the stairs when Zaylie hurried into the master bedroom to tell Chase and Toby she was leaving. She was rounding the corner to the bathroom when she slammed right into Chase. With a gasp, she jumped backward and quickly apologized.

"What were you doing, sneaking around the corner like that?" he demanded.

At the tone in his voice, Smutti put her tail down and let out a low growl. Chase glanced uncertainly at her, his eyes losing some of their fire.

"First of all, one doesn't sneak around one's own house," Zaylie retorted. "I was coming to tell you and Mr. Toby that I am going out for a while." Glancing over Chase's shoulder, she asked, "Where *is* Mr. Toby?"

"He had to run to the bank," Chase replied.

"Oh," Zaylie hesitated. "Well, I'll wait until he gets back."

His eyes narrowing, Chase asked, "What's the matter? You don't trust me to be in your house by myself?"

Zaylie had to bite her tongue to keep from telling him what his grandfather had told Gran. Instead, she stated, "I guess I just want to make sure I'm around in case you need any more flashlights."

Chase's crystal blue eyes glinted in anger at Zaylie's words and he took a small step forward, only to stop when Smutti growled again. With a tight smile, Zaylie spun around and left the room with Smutti at her side. She stood in the foyer and listened, and after a moment, she heard Chase get back to work.

CHAPTER 28

Azalea - 1966

After I left Cookie's house, I decided to go to Big Hal's. I wanted them both to know what was going on, and I wanted to see Big Hal's reaction when I asked about the sale of the bank. I only hoped Cookie hadn't already called and told him.

When I arrived at the Beecher mansion, the maid let me in. She seemed to be a bit frazzled with all the hurricane preparations and asked me to wait in the foyer until Mr. Beecher was available to see me.

After the maid hurried away, I suddenly heard voices coming from Big Hal's office. Tiptoeing over to the door that was pulled to, I peered through the crack and saw Mildred and Big Hal standing next to his desk. They were speaking in hissed whispers and by the look on both their faces, it wasn't a pleasant conversation.

"Once this is all over, we'll talk about it further," Big Hal stated.

With flashing eyes, Mildred said, "No, we'll talk about it now. How dare you think you could get away with this, Harold Beecher!"

Big Hal's jaw clenched tightly, and I could see his face turning red. "You can't begin to imagine the reason why, can you?" he hissed. "If so, you'd have to come to the conclusion that it's your fault, and you can't handle being responsible for anything."

Mildred gasped. "*My* fault?" she all but screeched. "Why, you pompous, arrogant..."

I could hear the sound of approaching footsteps, so I quickly backed away from the office door. What could Big Hal and Mildred possibly be arguing about? I knew that Mildred's extreme wealth often caused her to throw her weight around, and I'd questioned at times why Big Hal put up with it. I'd always thought it was because he was madly in love with her, but judging by the look of pure hatred on his face just now, I'd wager to say I was wrong.

"Azalea, what are you doing here?"

Pulling myself away from my thoughts, I looked at Dale Beecher and said, "I just stopped by to talk to your dad."

With a condescending smirk, he asked, "Come to whine about something else?"

"Something else?" I asked coolly, raising an eyebrow. "What exactly have I whined about before?"

"Any time you didn't get your way," he replied with a chuckle.

I looked at him in disgust, wondering why I ever bothered trying to carry on a conversation with him. He despised me, he always had, and the feeling was mutual.

Not bothering to respond further to his

attempts to annoy me, I asked, "Could you let your father know I'm here?"

Glancing toward the office, where the sound of angry voices was becoming louder and louder, Dale walked quickly toward the door and closed it.

"I'm afraid he can't see you right now," he said. "He just got an important call from Cookie and is, uh, in the middle of something."

Trying to maintain a neutral expression, I said, "I understand. Maybe once the storm has passed, I can stop back by then." I turned to leave but hesitated for a moment. Looking back at Dale, I boldly asked, "What did Sheriff Odin want to see you and Brenda about?"

Without batting an eye, he replied, "Why, he was questioning us about *you,* of course."

My eyes narrowing, I asked, "Oh? What kind of questions did he ask about me?"

Dale started to chuckle then, which caught me a bit off guard. "They weren't just about you," he replied. "He also wanted to know if we could confirm our whereabouts the night the bank was robbed."

"What did you tell him?" I asked.

"The truth," he stated.

I sighed inwardly, trying to control my temper. "So, you're not going to tell what was said about me?" I pressed.

"It's so bad that I'm not sure I should repeat what was said," he replied, and for once, I couldn't tell if he was serious.

"Fine," I ground out, my jaw clenched in irritation as I spun around and marched back out the front door.

Dale followed me and took a seat on one of the rocking chairs that had yet to be removed. He leaned his head back and closed his eyes, acting completely unfazed by the work going on around him as windows were boarded up and items were tied down. When he opened one eye and caught me staring, I flinched.

"Could either of you confirm your whereabouts the night the bank was robbed and Russell was killed?" I asked bluntly.

With a smirk, Dale simply rested his head back against the chair and closed his eyes. His pompous attitude and refusal to answer my question made me furious, and I stepped forward to...to what? Blowing out a quick, angry breath, I spun on my heel and hurried to my car. As I drove away, I glanced in the rearview mirror to see that Dale had stood up and was watching me leave.

When I got home, the wind was getting stronger and J.R. wasn't there yet. The clouds were getting heavier by the moment and I knew it was only a matter of time before the rain began, so I set about moving things into the house and shed. I dragged the rocking chairs inside, carried potted plants into the shed, and took down Mama's wind chimes. I made a note to ask J.R. to take down the porch swing and put it in the shed, and then I went inside to look through Papa's notebook once more. I was nervous and restless, and I wanted to make certain I hadn't missed anything.

I'd barely flipped through the first five pages when J.R. arrived. I went outside to show him what needed to be done, and as I helped him with the porch swing, I was surprised to see an unfamiliar car pull into my driveway.

"I didn't realize you were friends with the likes of her," J.R. commented.

Squinting through the growing shadows, I realized my visitor was Cookie and Cynthia's maid, Astrid.

"I didn't realize we were friends either," I murmured. Turning to look at J.R., I asked, "What do you mean by 'the likes of her'?"

J.R. simply shook his head and chuckled, making no effort to answer me as he carried the swing around to the shed. Astrid climbed from her car, clutching her purse tightly against her chest as she hurried toward me. I noticed she wore a worried expression on her face, and when she spotted me standing on the porch watching her, she hesitated.

"Uh, M-Miss Layne," she stammered. "I'm sorry to just stop by like this, but I overheard your conversation with Mr. Cook and I really need to talk to you. Can...can I come inside?"

Nodding, I opened the front door and motioned for her to come into the house. She was around my age, perhaps a year or two older, and very pretty.

Her cautious blue eyes darted back and forth as she followed me into the sitting room, as if expecting someone to jump out at her from behind the door. When she sat on the loveseat, her posture was stiff and rigid.

"What can I do for you?" I asked as I sat next to her.

"I..." she started and then stopped, glancing down at the floor as she murmured, "I can't believe I'm doing this."

"Doing *what*?" I questioned a bit impatiently.

Her gaze jerking upward, Astrid took a deep breath and said, "I need to give you something."

My brow furrowing with confusion, I watched as Astrid reached into her purse and pulled out a velvet pouch. She handed it to me, and when I loosened the drawstrings and looked inside, it felt as if every bit of air was sucked out of my lungs. Resting inside the pouch were the stolen diamonds.

CHAPTER 29

Zaylie

Looking up at Gran with wide eyes, Zaylie gasped, "Toby's wife stole the diamonds?"

Rubbing her temple, Gran shook her head in bewilderment. "I have a hard time believing that," she said.

Before they could continue, Gran's cell phone rang. Putting on her glasses, Gran looked at the screen and frowned. "It's Jan," she said. "What in the world is she doing calling so late?"

Zaylie sat and listened as Jan Booker, one of Gran's oldest friends, told her she was in the hospital.

"I fell, Lou. Can you believe it?" Jan sighed. "I was afraid I'd broken everything from my right shoulder down, but it looks like it's just my ankle. They're going to keep me until tomorrow, though, just to make sure."

After talking for a moment more, it was decided that Gran would go stay the night with her until Jan's daughter could arrive from Atlanta.

"Give Jan my best," Zaylie said later as she carried the overnight bag to Gran's car. "Are you sure you don't want me to drive you? I can pick you up tomorrow."

Giving her granddaughter a look, Gran stated tartly, "Don't be ridiculous. I'm more than capable of driving myself."

Holding up her hands in surrender, Zaylie said with a chuckle, "Okay, just be careful. Love you."

As Gran drove away, Zaylie went back inside, shaking her head. Her grandmother had always been feisty and independent, but Zaylie worried about her the older she got. Would Gran listen, though? No, she was just as stubborn as ever.

After taking a shower in her own bathroom since Ryker had gotten everything fixed, Zaylie drank a cup of chamomile tea and went to bed. She'd been asleep for nearly two hours when something woke her. Sitting up in bed, she listened for a moment, her mind still groggy from sleep.

Tap, tap, tap.

It was then that she realized it was Smutti pacing around the room. Leaning over, Zaylie clicked on the lamp beside her bed.

"What's wrong, girl?" she asked with a yawn. "Do you need to go outside?"

Walking over to the window, Smutti nudged the curtain with her nose and whined. Her brow furrowing, Zaylie climbed out of bed and walked over to the window to peer outside. At first, she didn't see anything, but as her eyes drifted around the dark yard, she suddenly noticed a large silhouette standing beneath the oak tree just outside her window. With a gasp, she jerked backward and dropped the curtain, letting it fall back in place.

What should I do? She thought, her heart racing. ***Call the police? Can they even get here in time?***

Taking a deep breath, Zaylie stepped forward once more and slid the curtain back, peering outside. The shadow was gone, and Zaylie wondered if she'd really seen it after all.

The next morning, Zaylie called Odin to tell him what happened...or what she thought happened.

"Did you check the cameras?" he wanted to know.

"Yes, but they didn't catch anything," she replied.

"So, you woke up in the middle of the night, saw a shadow standing beneath a tree, and then it was gone," he stated matter-of-factly. "Did you ever consider the fact that you may have been dreaming?"

Zaylie rolled her eyes. "I wasn't dreaming, Sheriff," she replied. "My dog sensed something, too."

"Uh-huh," was his reply. "Well, since there's nothing I can do, all I can say is to make sure you have your security system armed and the floodlights turned on each night."

"Thanks a lot," she said in a clipped tone before ending the call.

As Zaylie let Smutti outside, she saw that the construction crew was already hard at work and

Shawn Eaton was mowing the grass on the south side of the property. When he spotted her, he shut the mower off and hurried her way with a wave.

"Zaylie, can I talk to you for a minute?" he called out.

Nodding, Zaylie shaded her eyes from the sun and waited until he reached the back porch. She noticed that both Grady Young and Alan Whitlock stopped working and turned around to watch Shawn as he walked her way. They both said something to each other, and Zaylie wondered what it was. When they saw her looking, they quickly turned and got back to work.

"Hey, I wanted to know if it would be okay for me to cut back the azalea bushes along the driveway?" Shawn asked.

"Just as long as they'll still bloom during the spring," Zaylie replied with a smile.

They talked a bit more, and then Shawn asked how the investigation was going.

"I honestly don't know," she replied with a shrug. "Sheriff Carter won't keep me informed, so I have no idea if he's making any progress or not."

"Annoying old man, isn't he?" Shawn shook his head in disgust. "Seems like I know a lot of those."

Eyeing him, Zaylie asked, "You're referring to your grandfather, Dale Beecher?"

Shawn looked at her in surprise. "How did..." he paused as realization passed over his face. "Oh, Rita must have told you."

Zaylie nodded. "Yes, but I also saw your profile

216

picture on social media," she replied. "It must be hard for you to be estranged from your grandparents."

"Grandparents?" Shawn laughed. "My grandfather dumped my grandmother when I was three; he's had two other wives since. His current wife is thirty years younger than he is."

Zaylie raised her eyebrows in surprise. "So, do you ever see your grandmother?" she asked hesitantly.

"Once a year at Christmas, if I'm lucky," he replied with a shrug. "She's remarried now and living in New York."

He was bitter about the situation, that much was obvious. He'd had the opportunity to choose a different career, but for some reason, he'd decided not to.

"I'm sure it's hard, living on the same island as your grandfather," she said.

Shawn waved a hand in the air and said nonchalantly, "Nah, we run in different circles, so it's not like we ever bump into each other."

Zaylie could hear the doorbell ringing and realized that Mr. Toby and Chase must have arrived. Today was supposed to be their last day, and Zaylie was relieved. She was ready for things to start getting back to normal around the house, and the sooner Chase wasn't around anymore, the better.

Excusing herself, Zaylie called to Smutti and then hurried inside to let the two men in. As she opened the front door and stepped aside to give the men entrance, she noticed a long, bloody scratch running along Chase's forearm.

"You should really put something on that," she told him, eyeing the scratch.

Jerking his sleeve down over his arm, Chase smiled tightly and said, "Yeah, I'll do that. Being a plumber is tough work sometimes."

Zaylie noticed that Mr. Toby glanced back at his grandson with a furrowed brow, as if wondering what he was talking about. Zaylie didn't say anything further and left the two men alone, but she didn't think he'd gotten that scratch at work.

CHAPTER 30

Azalea - 1966

S lowly, I raised my eyes to stare at Astrid in complete and utter confusion. Shaking my head, I asked in a hoarse voice, "H-how did you get the diamonds?"

Twisting her hands nervously, Astrid jumped up from her place on the loveseat and began to pace back and forth in front of me. Her face was deathly pale, and I could tell she was fighting a war on the inside.

With a heavy sigh, Astrid turned to face me and the story finally began to flow from her trembling lips. I sat and listened, my eyes bulging wide with shock. I couldn't believe what she was telling me. Suddenly, a loud pounding sound met our ears, and we both jumped in surprise. I turned around in my seat, breathing a sigh of relief when I realized it was just J.R. boarding up the windows.

"I want you to take the diamonds to the police and tell them everything," Astrid stated.

"Astrid, they're not going to believe me," I told her. "You'll have to tell them, not me."

Taking a step back, Astrid shook her head vehemently and said, "*No.* I'm sorry, but I just can't do that. You'll have to figure something out."

With that, she turned and hurried from the room. I ran after her and tried to give the diamonds back, but she pushed them away. With wild eyes, she hissed, "I can't ruin my life. Go to the sheriff, or take the diamonds and disappear. Either way, I wash my hands of it, and if you tell Odin of my involvement, I'll deny everything." Hesitating, she quickly glanced around before adding in a low tone, "Whatever you do, just watch your back, Miss Layne."

As Astrid jumped into her car and sped away, the clouds broke and the first bands of rain began. I rushed back underneath the cover of the porch and watched as her car rounded the bend and disappeared. It wasn't until then that I noticed J.R. Whitlock peering around the corner, watching me. When our eyes met, he smiled slightly and then got back to work. Had he overheard our conversation?

Tucking the pouch of diamonds beneath my arm, I walked into the house and shut the door behind me. I stood in the foyer for a moment, my thoughts racing. The same question, however, kept repeating itself over and over in my mind.

What now?

I had been pacing around my living room for the last hour, trying to decide what to do. J.R. was almost finished with the house, and I was glad; the weather was getting worse, and the sooner he left, the better.

The clock on the mantle seemed to tick louder than normal as if reminding me that time was running out. What should I do? If I tried to explain everything to Odin, he wouldn't believe me. Or would he? Perhaps J.R. would say he saw Astrid at my house, and if he'd really overheard part of our conversation, he may back me up on that, too.

Oh, if only I could ask for someone's advice! Louella was already at her future in-laws' house and Toby...

That's it! I could ask Toby for help; I knew I could trust him. Rushing over to the telephone, I quickly dialed his number.

"Hello?"

The line was filled with static; the storm was already affecting the island.

"Toby, it's Azalea," I said, hoping he could hear me. "I need to talk to you about something. Can you come over to the house?"

"Right now?" he asked.

"Yes," I replied. "Can you?"

"Is it an emergency?" he wanted to know. "I'm trying to get my house ready for the storm. It's last minute, I know, but I've been too busy to do it until now. I'm about to help Dad put out some sandbags; he and Mom are staying with me until the storm blows over."

I heaved a sigh. "No, I guess it's not an emergency," I replied. "It can wait. Good luck with the storm."

Some friend he is, I thought as I slammed the phone back down onto the receiver. If Louella had been the one to call, he'd have dropped everything and gone running to her.

I stomped around the living room for a moment more until I finally decided to go down to the police station. I would talk to Odin first to sort of feel him out and show him Papa's notebook along with the note I'd found in Big Hal's office. I wouldn't tell him *where* I'd found it, of course, and perhaps it wouldn't matter, anyway.

By the time I drove away from the house, the wind was howling through the trees, blowing leaves and Spanish moss all across my path. The rain was thick and heavy, and I had to turn my windshield wipers on to the highest speed to be able to see enough to drive. Perhaps I should have waited until the storm passed, but I felt an urgency down deep in my soul to do it now. It was now or never.

I had to drive slowly and carefully, as the heavy rain was already starting to flood the streets. When I finally made it to the station and ran inside the building, I was soaked. The building was eerily quiet, and for a moment, I thought no one was there.

"Miss Layne?"

I turned to see one of the younger officers peering around the corner, looking at me with a surprised expression.

"Is Sheriff Odin here?" I asked.

The officer shook his head and said, "No, ma'am, I'm afraid not. Is there anything I can help you with?"

I hesitated, my heart pounding. Dare I confide in this young man? After a moment, I squared my shoulders and said, "No, thank you."

As I ran back through the rain toward my car, I knew that I'd found my answer. This storm was my chance to escape, and once the night fell, I would disappear for good...with the diamonds.

CHAPTER 31

Zaylie

Zaylie stared at the final written page of the diary in confusion. Azalea planned to run off with the diamonds, that much was obvious, but what happened?

"I can't believe she was really going to do it," Gran breathed.

"Gran, what do you think Astrid told her?" Zaylie asked.

Gran sighed and shook her head. "I don't know, and I guess we never will," she replied. "As you already know, Astrid died years ago."

"Do...do you think Mr. Toby knows?" Zaylie asked hesitantly.

Gran frowned at her granddaughter. "No, of course not," she stated indignantly. "I don't believe he would have married her if he'd known she was somehow involved in a crime. Are you sure that's the end of the diary? There's nothing more?"

Zaylie shook her head, wishing Azalea had finished the story. Now, they may never know what happened.

Her eyes drifting down to the bottom of the last page, Zaylie said, "Well, there's a P.S. written here, but I can't make any sense of it."

"What does it say?" Grab wanted to know.

"If you want to know the truth, listen for the sound of the red pecker."

Gran's brow furrowed. "We used to tell Azalea the red-bellied woodpeckers that would nest in her mother's birdhouses looked like her because of the red hair," she said. "I have no idea, though, what that has to do with anything."

Zaylie closed the book and sighed. "Me neither." They lapsed into a deep silence, both lost in their own thoughts. After a moment, Zaylie announced she was going to bed. Standing, she stretched and went over to kiss Gran good night. As she and Smutti headed upstairs, Zaylie found herself wishing there was someone still alive who could tell them what really happened.

As Zaylie stepped into her bedroom and flipped on the light, she paused. There **was** someone who could possibly confirm it: J R. Whitlock. Alan said he would go with her to visit his father sometime this week. Would the old man tell the truth? Was he even mentally capable of doing so? Zaylie wasn't sure, but she was anxious to give it another try.

The next morning, Zaylie received a call from her manager, Leslie, at the training center in Crescent Moon, Tennessee.

"I hate to bother you, but we've got a problem," Leslie said. "One of our employees quit yesterday, another is on vacation, and two more are out sick. We're drowning over here, Zaylie. What should we do?"

"I'm on my way," Zaylie said as she grabbed her purse and headed to the kitchen to tell Gran. "I should be there a little after noon and I'll stay as long as you need me."

"Thank you," Leslie said, and Zaylie could hear the relief in her voice.

After telling Gran the news, Zaylie decided to leave Smutti at home. She didn't like the idea of Gran staying by herself right now with everything that had happened and felt better knowing Smutti was with her.

"I'll call you as soon as I get there," Zaylie promised, knowing how Gran worried about her.

She grabbed some snacks and drinks from the kitchen and then headed out. As she drove, she wondered how it was going to work owning two training centers. Obviously, she couldn't be in two places at once, and for the first time since moving back to Whisper Island, she started to feel worried. Leslie was a great manager and usually kept things under control, but what would happen if both centers had an emergency at the same time?

Zaylie's thoughts were so filled with worry that she didn't immediately notice her brakes weren't as sensitive as usual. She'd driven for nearly thirty minutes on the interstate without having to brake much at all, but when a semi pulled into her lane and she tapped the pedal, her car barely slowed down at all. She pushed harder, and when nothing happened, her heart rate shot through the roof when she realized something was terribly wrong. She was going nearly eighty miles per hour, she was currently in the middle lane surrounded by traffic, and her brakes weren't working.

Her car was getting closer and closer to the semi, and Zaylie quickly checked her surroundings. Several cars were to her right, preventing her from getting over into the emergency lane. There was also a truck coming up behind her. She would have to use the emergency brake, but if she didn't time everything just right, she could cause a major accident.

Turning on her emergency flashing lights, she moved into the left-hand lane, her fingers turning white as she clutched the steering wheel. If she could get around the semi, she'd have a clear path to veer all the way over into the emergency lane. Taking a deep breath, she put her foot on the gas and pressed. Her car began to go faster and faster, and Zaylie fought against the panic that caused little droplets of sweat to form on her brow. If this didn't go according to plan, she was going to die.

She was past the semi now; it was time to bring this car to a stop. With her flashers still on, she veered over and over until she finally reached the emergency lane. The sound of her tires striking the rumble strips was like fingernails on a chalkboard. With trembling fingers, she gently pressed the emergency brake. Trucks and cars flew by her, blowing their horns as Zaylie fought to maintain control of her car as it began to slow down. Sweat dripped down her neck and into her eyes, but she tried to stay focused.

The time that lapsed was only a matter of seconds, but it seemed to pass in slow motion. When her car finally came to a stop, Zaylie sat in silence for a moment, her fingers glued to the steering wheel. Her entire body shook as the adrenaline began to wear off, and after taking a few deep breaths, Zaylie sat back against the seat and tried to gather her thoughts. What had happened? Why had her brakes failed?

Zaylie finally got herself together and called a towing company. She then called Leslie to let her know what happened and that she wouldn't be able to make it as soon as she'd thought.

"Zaylie, you could have been killed!" Leslie gasped. "Look, don't worry about coming up here. I was actually about to call and ask your opinion on something, anyway. What if I asked Myles to come out and help for the next few days?"

Zaylie raised her eyebrows in surprise. Myles was Leslie's ex-husband, and the two hadn't parted on good terms.

"Are you sure you're comfortable with that?" Zaylie asked.

Leslie blew out a breath. "Desperate times call for desperate measures," she replied with a chuckle. "He's a good trainer, and I don't want you to have to worry about driving all the way here.

Especially after what you've been through today."

"Okay, but let me know if it doesn't work out," Zaylie said. "I can get a rental and come up tomorrow."

Not long after they hung up, the tow truck arrived and took Zaylie back to the island. When she arrived at the mechanic shop, she went into the waiting room and called Gran. She didn't tell her just how bad the situation had been; she simply said her brakes went out and she was waiting at Larry's Garage.

Twenty minutes later, Larry came inside to give Zaylie the news. She wasn't prepared, though, to hear what he had to say.

"Zaylie," he said, his voice filled with concern as he wiped his hands on a rag, "your brake line was cut."

CHAPTER 32

Zaylie

After recovering from the initial shock of Larry's discovery, Zaylie immediately called Sheriff Carter. He came down to the garage to talk to Larry and look over the car first, then he joined Zaylie in the waiting room.

"Larry is right," he told her. "The brake lines were definitely cut. I'd say they weren't cut all the way through, though, which is why the brakes worked a little at first."

"Could you check for fingerprints?"

Odin shook his head. "I doubt it; there's too much cross-contamination. Who has had access to your car in the last few days?" he wanted to know.

"Pretty much anyone who's been on the property," she replied. "I left it parked on the driveway for a couple of days because Gran was cleaning out the garage and I wanted her to have some extra room." Zaylie stopped and blinked as a thought crossed her mind. "Sheriff, I'll bet that man I saw standing outside my window two nights ago is responsible."

"The man you *thought* you saw," he stated

Pursing her lips, Zaylie replied, "I'd say the cut brake lines are a testament to what I saw, as I doubt anyone would do something like that in broad daylight."

Odin cleared his throat and stood up. "Well, I'll have my guys dust the car for fingerprints, but like I said, I doubt they'll find anything."

"Please let me know one way or another," Zaylie told him, and he nodded in agreement.

"Would you like a ride home?" he asked.

Surprised at the kind gesture, Zaylie said, "My rental won't be delivered until later today, so yes, I would appreciate a ride. Thank you."

As Odin drove in the direction of Azalea Bluff, Zaylie tried to make small talk, but the elderly man barely grunted out his replies. Finally, she lapsed into silence, and after a moment, he asked, "So, what's this I hear about you and Louella finding some diary or something of Azalea's?"

Zaylie's eyes widened, and she shifted uncomfortably in her seat. "Uh, yes, we stumbled upon a diary of hers," she replied nonchalantly.

Glancing over at her, Odin asked, "Is there anything in it I need to know about?"

Zaylie hesitated. What should she do? Gran hadn't said whether she'd changed her mind about sharing the contents of the diary with Sheriff Carter or not. If Zaylie went ahead and told him, Gran would have her head. She couldn't lie either, though.

With a sigh, Zaylie said cautiously, "There are a few...questionable entries."

"If it has anything to do with her murder, you'd

better give it to me," he replied in a firm tone. "Withholding evidence is a crime, Miss Layne."

Zaylie swallowed past the growing lump in her throat. "I'll, uh, talk it over with Gran," she replied. "Give us a couple of days?"

Odin sighed. "It goes against my better judgment," he stated, "but okay."

When they arrived at Azalea Bluff, Zaylie thanked Sheriff Carter for the ride and hurried inside before he changed his mind about the diary. She searched the house for Gran and finally found her sitting on the back deck with Smutti as the two watched the construction crew.

"Oh, honey, I'm so glad you're okay!" Gran cried as she jumped to her feet and pulled Zaylie into a hug. "I can't believe you didn't tell me the whole story."

Surprised, Zaylie pulled back and asked, "Who *did* tell you?"

"Toby called and told me," she replied as she pushed Zaylie into a nearby rocking chair.

"How did he know?" Zaylie frowned.

"I don't know," Gran replied with a shrug. "I suppose Larry told him."

Zaylie shook her head. "Oh, the joys of living in a small town," she muttered as she absentmindedly rubbed Smutti behind the ears.

"Does Odin have any clue who could be responsible for trying to kill you?" Gran wanted to know.

"He said they would check the car for

fingerprints," Zaylie replied, "but he was doubtful they'd find anything."

Gran sighed. "This is getting out of hand," she stated.

Biting her lower lip, Zaylie said hesitantly, "He wants us to give him the diary, Gran. He said that withholding evidence is a crime."

"We're not withholding evidence because there's nothing written in that diary that says who killed Azalea," Gran stated. "I don't want him, or anyone else for that matter, to know that she was planning to run off with those diamonds."

"I don't imagine Mr. Toby would be too happy either since his wife was also supposedly involved," Zaylie replied with a sigh.

"Exactly," Gran said, nodding. "I don't trust Odin Carter not to leak those rumors. If Toby found out I was the one who gave Odin that information, he'd never forgive me."

"So, what do we do?" Zaylie asked.

Gran thought it over for a moment. "I'll talk to Odin," she finally said. "If he refuses to cooperate, we'll go see a lawyer."

Zaylie nodded, and the two lapsed into silence as they sat on the deck and watched the crew work. A couple of hours later, Zaylie's phone rang, and her heart caught when she saw Micah's name flashing across the screen.

"Zaylie, I heard what happened," he said as soon as she answered. "Are you okay?"

"Yes, I'm fine," she replied with a smile. "Thanks

for checking on me."

Clearing his throat, Micah said, "After what you've been through, I thought it might do you some good to get out and do something fun. It has nothing to do with the water," he quickly added. "I promise."

With a laugh, Zaylie asked, "What did you have in mind?"

"Dinner and a movie?" he asked. "That new drive-in theater is open; I thought it would be fun to check it out."

"That sounds really nice," she replied.

"Pick you up at six?"

She agreed, and after they hung up, she felt butterflies dancing in her stomach.

Micah picked Zaylie up at six o'clock sharp and took her to one of the best seafood restaurants on the island. She wore a three-quarter sleeve blue dress with white flowers, and her auburn hair hung loosely around her shoulders.

"You look beautiful tonight, by the way," Micah said after they were seated.

"Thanks," she replied with a smile. "You look great, too."

She wasn't lying about her compliment. He wore a pair of khaki pants and a hunter-green button-up shirt that was rolled up to his elbows. She couldn't help but notice how well his shoulders filled out the shirt, and she felt her cheeks grow warm when he smiled at her.

The food was delicious, and as they ate, Zaylie suddenly noticed two familiar faces in the crowd. They were sitting in a far corner that was a bit hidden from the rest of the room, but she wasn't mistaken: it was Shawn Eaton and his grandfather, Dale Beecher.

"That's strange," she muttered. When Micah looked at her questioningly, she nodded in the direction of the table and said, "I was under the impression that those two were estranged."

Micah's brow furrowed as he turned to look at the two men. "You and me both," he replied. "I'm very surprised to see them together."

Zaylie watched the two for a while, noticing that their conversation seemed a little intense. When the server approached their table and they immediately stopped talking, Zaylie wondered what they had been discussing.

"Shall we get to that movie, or would you rather stay here and snoop for a while?" Micah asked with a chuckle.

Pulling her attention away from Shawn and Dale, Zaylie smiled and said, "Let's go."

The new drive-in theater was next to the beach, which allowed the viewers to roll down their windows if they wished and enjoy a nice breeze. The theater was surprisingly full for a mid-week night, and Micah parked three rows back.

"I've never been to a drive-in movie before," Micah stated as he turned his radio to the correct station. With a grin, he added, "It's a little cozy, isn't it?"

Her cheeks flushing, Zaylie nodded her head in agreement. Glancing over at the car next to theirs, she was a bit taken aback by the intense gaze that stared back at her. Chase Garner was parked beside them, and it seemed he had come to the movie alone. Throwing up her hand in a small wave, Zaylie smiled at him but he simply looked away with no response.

"He's a bit of an odd character, if you ask me," Micah stated.

Looking back at her date, Zaylie said, "Tell me about it. His grandfather is so nice, but I'm afraid I can't say the same about Chase. Honestly, the way he was looking at me just now kind of gave me the creeps."

Pushing the console out of the way, Micah said, "Slide away from the window, if you want. I certainly don't mind."

Zaylie pushed herself away from the window and closer to Micah. He smiled warmly at her, and as the sun sank over the ocean and the movie began to play, Zaylie sighed happily. After all these years, and regardless of the hurt he'd put her through, she'd missed Micah.

Halfway through the movie, Micah's phone rang and he started to climb from the car to answer. Putting her hand on his arm, Zaylie said she was going to the concession stand to grab some snacks.

"Want anything?" she asked just before he

answered the call.

"You know what I like," he replied, his eyes twinkling.

With a smile, Zaylie hurried through the rows of cars and over to the concession stand. She grabbed herself a bag of yogurt-covered pretzels and a Sprite, and as she tried to decide what to get Micah, she felt a presence step up behind her.

"Hi, Zaylie."

Turning, Zaylie smiled politely at Chase and said, "Hi. Here by yourself?"

His friendly expression turned sour at her question, and he snapped, "Is that such a bad thing?"

Raising her eyebrows, Zaylie shook her head and replied, "No, not at all."

"I suppose I could have asked *you* to come with me, but I see you have your eyes on a much bigger prize," he stated cynically.

Zaylie blinked. "Excuse me?" she asked. "A bigger prize?"

Chase smirked. "You people are all the same," he said. "The rich can only marry the rich."

Zaylie's eyes narrowed. "I wouldn't exactly call myself rich," she retorted. "I've worked very hard for the things I have. Furthermore, Micah and I are not getting married. We're not even dating."

"Oh, you worked for that mansion of a house on Azalea Bluff?" Chase chortled.

Before she could reply, he leaned over her, his much larger frame covering hers. Zaylie drew in a quick breath of surprise and pushed herself against the counter, her heart picking up speed.

"Don't worry," he said in a low voice, his breath hot against her face, "I'm only getting a drink."

With that being said, he slapped his money on the counter, grabbed a Coke, and sauntered off. Zaylie watched as his shadow melted into the darkness and swallowed past the lump in her throat. Why did he always seem to put her on guard?

Sighing, Zaylie grabbed a drink and bag of Chex Mix for Micah, paid for the snacks, and hurried back to the car.

"I was starting to worry," Micah said when she returned, his eyes lighting up when he saw what she'd gotten for him. "How much do I owe you?"

Zaylie waved a hand in the air. "You paid for dinner, so snacks are on me." Glancing over at Chase's car, she told Micah what happened and said, "I guess I'm just a little edgy."

"I think he was probably just trying to flirt and failed miserably," Micah said as he took a sip of his drink. Eyeing Zaylie for a moment, he asked, "So, you told him we aren't dating, huh?"

Zaylie glanced at him in surprise. "Well...yes," she stammered.

Reaching over to take her hand, he said in a soft voice, "We could always change that."

Zaylie hesitated as a million thoughts began to race through her mind. The night was dark, and as the movie played, shadows flickered across Micah's face. They were sitting close, only inches apart, and at the exact moment the characters on the screen kissed, Micah leaned forward.

Zaylie felt a wave of emotion engulf her as Micah's lips covered hers. He'd kissed her many times when they were dating before, but that was so long ago and so much had changed...or had it? Had her feelings really changed that much? She couldn't tell, not now, not with the way his touch made her forget every doubt she'd ever had.

"I've missed you," he whispered as he reached up to tuck a strand of hair behind her ear. Leaning back, his beautiful blue eyes were filled with emotion as he asked, "Do you feel the same?"

Zaylie nodded; it was all she could do at the moment. With a warm smile, Micah wrapped an arm around her waist and pulled her closer. Resting her head on his shoulder as they watched the ending of the movie, Zaylie sighed.

Once the movie was over and they started to drive away, Zaylie glanced out her window once more. Chase had his window rolled down and was watching them with a triumphant look on his face.

CHAPTER 33

Zaylie

Micah drove Zaylie home and walked her to the door. The night was humid but cool, and the crickets seemed to be singing louder than usual.

"Zaylie, I know we can't go back to the way we were," Micah said, his voice soft and smooth in the night, "but I want you to know that I still care about you. Would...would you be willing to give me another chance? To give *us* another chance?"

Zaylie couldn't believe she was standing at the threshold of what could possibly lead to another relationship with Micah Pierce. Suddenly, she felt like a teenager again; butterflies danced in her stomach, and Micah's hand on her arm made her knees weak. At the same time, the weight of the years that had passed seemed to settle on her shoulders, reminding her of everything she'd been through. How she could feel so young and old all at once was a little overwhelming...and confusing.

As if sensing the inward battle she was fighting, Micah pulled her into his arms, pressing her head against his chest. Zaylie could hear the soft beating of his heart against her ear, and she slowly began to relax. After a moment, she pulled back to look up at him and found that his face was only inches from hers. He closed the space between them and kissed her once again, his lips warm against hers. She wrapped her arms firmly around his neck, pulling him closer as the pounding of their hearts blended together to create one rhythm.

Moments later, Zaylie pulled back and said softly, "My answer is yes. I'd like to give us another chance."

She could see Micah's smile through the shadows, and she hoped she'd made the right decision. She hadn't given herself time to think it through, but she still cared for Micah. She knew that much.

After Micah left, Zaylie went inside and climbed up to bed. It had been a long day, and she was exhausted. When she tried to sleep, though, all she could do was lie awake and think about Micah.

The next day, Gran packed an overnight bag to take over to her friend Jan's house. Her daughter, it seemed, had to go back to Atlanta for a couple of days, and Gran had agreed to stay with Jan until her daughter returned.

"Are you sure you can see about her by yourself?" Zaylie asked worriedly.

"You know how tiny Jan is," Gran replied as she walked toward the garage. "It won't be hard for me to help her get around. I'll be careful, though, I promise."

"Okay," Zaylie said, kissing her on the cheek. "Give Jan my best. See you in a few days!"

After Gran left, Zaylie spent the day doing paperwork and answering emails. Being the owner of a business wasn't an easy job, and she hoped she'd be able to manage two centers once the new one was complete.

It was well after five o'clock when Zaylie took a break from work and went outside with Smutti. She was surprised to see Alan Whitlock and his crew were still there; they were usually gone by now. The training center was coming along nicely, and Zaylie could hardly wait for it to be finished.

Smutti was sniffing around the yard but stopped when she spotted Grady Young walking toward the house. Her golden eyes watched his every step, and she quickly moved to stand at Zaylie's side.

"Hi, Grady," Zaylie greeted the young man as she leaned over to pet the protective dog.

"Afternoon," he replied with a nod. "Mr. Whitlock wanted me to tell you we're almost finished for the day."

"Thanks," she replied with a smile. "Y'all sure are getting a lot done."

Wiping sweat from his brow, Grady nodded and said, "Yes, ma'am, we work fast. Any updates from the sheriff on who might've killed your great aunt?"

Zaylie blinked, surprised at the sudden change in subject. "Uh, no, not really," she stumbled. "Honestly, though, I doubt we'll ever know what really happened."

Grady eyed her for a second before saying, "Maybe when Bill Harper takes back over, he'll be able to get more done. Odin Carter is too old, not that his age was an issue before. I guess he's just incompetent."

Zaylie tended to agree, but she didn't say so. Instead, she asked, "Do you think he's the reason the case wasn't solved the first time?"

"From what I've heard, it was a pretty open and shut case," Grady stated. "So, yes, I suppose it was his fault."

Zaylie wasn't sure what he meant about it being an open and shut case, but before she could ask him, Alan called out and Grady hurried back to work. As Zaylie watched him walk away, she wondered what Rita saw in him, even if they were just friends.

Just before the construction crew left, Alan Whitlock knocked on the back door.

"If you still want to talk to my father, I can meet you at his house in an hour," he told her.

Zaylie readily agreed, and once he was gone, she hurried upstairs to take a shower. A text message came through as she began to undress, and she smiled when she saw it was from Micah.

"How's my girl?"

Zaylie's heart fluttered at his words. She hadn't told Gran about them yet; she was still trying to process it herself.

Zaylie texted him back, asking about his day, and then jumped into the shower. Once she got out, she went downstairs and quickly fixed herself a sandwich, fed Smutti, and took her outside again. After everything was done, it was time to go. She grabbed her phone and purse and hurried out to her rental car.

Zaylie was halfway to Mr. Whitlock's house when her father called. She hadn't told him yet about her brake lines being cut, and he nearly went through the roof when she shared what happened.

"Honey, you'd better be careful," he told her. "This guy is liable to try again. You know what, I think I'll hire a bodyguard for you; I know a guy in Savannah."

"Dad, stop." Zaylie laughed. "You are not hiring me a bodyguard. I'll be careful, and I have Smutti; she'll protect me."

"Smutti can't protect you from cut brake lines," her dad stated drolly.

"Look, I'm sure this is all going to be over soon," Zaylie assured him. "I'm actually heading to J.R. Whitlock's house right now; I think he can help clear up some things."

"Zaylie, that man is crazy," her dad cried. "Have you lost your mind? You don't need to go out there by yourself."

"Calm down," Zaylie interrupted. "I'm not going by myself; I'm meeting Alan there. He promised to help me talk to his dad."

"You still need to be careful," he said in a disapproving tone.

Hoping to change the subject, Zaylie asked, "Did you hear that Russell Madison's great-nephew has moved back to the island? He's been working at the house with Alan's crew."

"Really?" her dad asked in surprise. "No, I didn't know that. I'm surprised any of that family would move back to Whisper Island."

"Gran said the same thing," Zaylie replied as she turned down J.R. Whitlock's driveway. "Mr. Toby's grandson has also been working at the house."

"Chase Garner?"

"You remember him?" Zaylie asked, slowing her car down a bit on the bumpy road.

"I remember hearing he was in prison for a few years," her dad replied.

Stopping the car in front of Mr. Whitlock's house, Zaylie raised her eyebrows in surprise and asked, "What was he in prison for?"

"I believe it was for breaking and entering, and also theft."

Zaylie sat back in shock, her eyes wide. Did Mr. Toby know his grandson had been in prison? She couldn't imagine that he would have kept that from Gran. On the other hand, some people on the island wouldn't want him working in their homes if they knew he'd been caught stealing.

"Who told you this, Dad?" Zaylie asked.

"You remember that lawyer I dated after your mom and I divorced, right?" her dad asked. "Well, she was affiliated with the prison he was in, and when she saw on his record that he was from Whisper Island, she asked if I knew him."

While her dad talked, Zaylie saw Alan Whitlock pull in beside her. "Hey, let me call you back," she told her dad, waving to Alan. "I want to hear more of this story."

"Okay, honey," he replied. "Be careful at old Mr. Whitlock's house."

Zaylie promised she would and then climbed out of the car. The sun was going down, and the thick woods surrounding Mr. Whitlock's house made it appear even darker than it was. Zaylie glanced around, wondering where the vicious Rottweiler was. With a shiver, she rubbed her arms and stepped closer to Alan's truck.

"Sorry I was late," he said as he climbed from his truck. "My ex called and wanted to argue about alimony. Sometimes I wonder how I stayed married to that woman as long as I did."

Zaylie smiled slightly but didn't say anything. She didn't remember much about Alan's ex-wife, except that she'd always tried living above their means. It seemed she was still trying to do so.

The house was dark when they entered, except for one light filtering in from the living room. As soon as they walked through the front door, Zaylie was struck by the overwhelming smell that lingered in the air. It was a mixture of dog urine, body odor, and the familiar mustiness that a home gets when it's never aired out. Shoes, books, boxes, and all manner of junk lay scattered along the floor. Zaylie spotted several roaches darting in and out of the clutter, and she felt her stomach turn.

"I wondered if you'd be brave enough to come back."

The now-familiar gruff voice that filtered through the shadows from the living room sent chills down Zaylie's spine. She peered around the doorframe and saw J.R. Whitlock sitting on the sofa with the giant Rottweiler next to him. They both stared at her through beady, suspicious eyes, and Zaylie hesitated just inside the doorway.

"It's okay, Miss Layne," Alan said, motioning for her to follow him into the messy room. "The dog won't bother you."

Unless the old man gives him the signal, Zaylie thought.

Taking a deep breath, she walked along the small path on the floor and stopped a few feet from J.R. and his dog. Piles of junk lined either side of her, and she suddenly felt her claustrophobia starting to raise its ugly head.

"Mr. W-Whitlock, I...uh," Zaylie stammered, pausing to clear her throat. "I know you were at Azalea's home the day she disappeared. Astrid Garner stopped by to see her. Do you remember?"

Mr. Whitlock stared at her in silence for a moment, the shadows cast by the lamp playing along the gaunt lines of his face. Raising a Styrofoam cup he held in one hand, he spat a string of tobacco into it.

"That was the year we nearly got wiped out by that dang hurricane," he stated.

Zaylie nodded. "Yes. Yes, that's right. You were at the house to board up the windows."

J.R. reached up a bony hand to wipe a bit of spittle from his gnarly beard. "You ain't got to tell me that, girl. I remember."

Zaylie swallowed, trying to gather her courage. Why did she feel so threatened and intimidated by this old man? Alan was there to protect her... wasn't he? She glanced over at Alan, hoping she was right. He stood there silently, watching his father.

Looking back at the old man, Zaylie squared her shoulders and said bluntly, "You overheard the conversation Azalea had with Astrid. Didn't you?"

A sneer curled Mr. Whitlock's lip, and he said, "Of course I did."

Her heart catching, Zaylie asked, "And? What did they say?"

Suddenly, the old man started to laugh. Looking at Alan, he said, "Seems like she wants something from me, son. Should I give it to her for free? Or should we make her pay?"

Zaylie looked at Alan, expecting him to set his father straight. What she saw instead sent off warning bells in her mind. Alan's eyes were gleaming, and with a smirk, he looked at her and said in a low voice, "I think we should make her pay."

CHAPTER 34

Zaylie

Her brow lowering in confusion, Zaylie asked, "Excuse me?"

"You can start with those diamonds," Alan replied. "Don't you think that would be good enough, Dad?"

"I think so." J.R. nodded in agreement.

"I-I don't have them," Zaylie stammered as she slowly took a step back.

His eyes glittering in the lamplight, Alan said, "I guess we'll just have to find them ourselves then."

Zaylie looked back and forth between the two men, trying to read their expressions. Was this some sort of joke? If it was, why did she suddenly feel so nervous?

"I think I'd like to go home now," she stated, turning to leave the room.

She didn't get very far. Before she could even take two steps, Alan's firm grip on her arm stopped her. Spinning around to face him, Zaylie said in a cool tone, "I don't know what's going on here, Mr. Whitlock, but it's not funny. Let go of my arm right now."

J.R. made a clicking sound with his tongue, and the Rottweiler jumped to his feet and began to bark viciously. With a gasp, Zaylie went completely still, but her heart pounded like a runaway train within her chest.

"I think you'd better calm down or ole Goliath is going to really get upset," Alan said in a deadly tone. "Now, I'll let go of your arm, but only if you promise not to make any sudden moves."

Zaylie nodded, and old Mr. Whitlock signaled for Goliath to stand down. Alan released her arm, and she stood there silently, watching them all with cautious eyes. She'd worked with dogs for nearly twenty years; she knew their behaviors and what could cause them to attack if triggered. She wasn't as adept at judging people, though, and she knew she needed to calm herself down and carefully assess the situation.

"What exactly do you want from me?" she asked in a low tone.

"I thought we'd made that clear," Alan replied.

Calmly, Zaylie stated, "I already told you I don't have the diamonds, nor do I know where they are."

Alan raised his eyebrows and replied in a similarly calm tone, "Then I guess you're of no use to us, which is what I've been trying to tell Dad all along."

Zaylie's eyes narrowed. "You're the one who tampered with my brakes?" she wanted to know.

Another smirk crossed Alan's face as he nodded. "I figured it'd be easier to search for the diamonds if you were out of the way."

Zaylie couldn't believe it. Alan Whitlock had run

a reputable company on the island for years, and she'd hired him in good faith to build her training center. People trusted him; *she'd* trusted him! How could he be the one responsible for trying to kill her?

"You're also the one who broke into the house and cut the power off?" she asked in a choked voice.

"I was after the diary that night," he replied. "I'd heard about it around town and figured it might have some information on where those diamonds are hidden. I thought I'd be able to run in and find it with no trouble, but that didn't work out, did it?"

"Why didn't you just kill me then?" she asked in bewilderment.

Alan glanced away. "I wasn't at that point just yet," he mumbled. His jaw clenching in anger, he added, "I didn't realize then just how much in debt I was, but my ex-wife reminded me of a few bills I'd forgotten about."

"Enough of all this jabbering," J.R. spoke up in an annoyed tone. "Get it over with, Alan."

Zaylie looked between the two of them as a feeling of trepidation crept up her spine. "Get on with *what*?" she demanded. "My father knows I'm here, and if any harm comes to me, he'll see that you both go to prison."

"But it'll be an accident," Alan said, the gleam coming back into his eyes. "You entered the house before I arrived, and Goliath was just doing what he's supposed to do."

251

Zaylie looked down at the dog, her stomach sinking. Goliath had obviously been trained to attack when told, and judging by the breadth of his chest and the solid, muscular frame, he'd tear her apart in minutes.

Trying to remain calm, Zaylie looked back at Alan and asked in a smooth voice, "What if I agreed to give you the diamonds?"

Alan's eyebrows shot up. "I thought you didn't have them?"

Zaylie smiled coyly. "I don't, yet, but I found something in the back of Azalea's diary. It's a small piece of paper, but I think it's a clue where the diamonds are hidden. I brought it with me to show Mr. Whitlock in the hope that he could decipher what it means…"

As she spoke, she opened her purse, as if looking for the paper. In reality, she was retrieving the small canister of pepper spray, and when she found it, her heart quickened.

"Here it is," she said, and as Alan leaned in for a closer look, she jerked the canister out of her purse and sprayed him directly in the face.

Alan jerked back with a scream of surprise and covered his eyes. Goliath barked and jumped up, ready to charge, but Zaylie acted quickly. With every ounce of strength she could muster, she shoved Alan directly into Goliath's path, throwing the dog off balance.

Spinning on her heel, Zaylie ran frantically from the living room and toward the front door. The house was so dark that she continuously tripped over the mounds of clutter all over the floor, but she managed to keep her footing. She could hear Goliath barking and the men yelling, but she didn't stop. Once she reached the front door, she threw it open, raced onto the front porch, and slammed the door shut behind her.

The night was eerily quiet; it was like the earth had stopped turning and life no longer existed. Zaylie's heart thundered in her chest as she hurried over to her car and grabbed the door handle. When it wouldn't open, she hesitated in confusion. It was then that she realized the rental car wasn't a keyless entry.

The front door banged open, and knowing she didn't have time to dig through her purse to find the car keys, Zaylie spun around and ran into the woods.

"Get her, Goliath!" Alan yelled, and Zaylie could hear the dog's nails skittering across the porch as he raced after her.

As Zaylie ran blindly through the dark woods, overgrown bushes slapped at her skin, leaving scratches and cuts all over her arms and legs. She shoved branches out of her way and leaped over fallen logs. She was heading toward the main road, and if she could make it before Goliath reached her, maybe someone would be driving by and stop to help.

She could hear the massive Rottweiler's mighty paws pounding the forest floor as he pursued her.

She pushed herself to go faster, but it was almost impossible to navigate through such a thick black forest. Her chest heaved and the sound of her own labored breathing nearly drowned out the pounding of her heart. She was getting tired and didn't think she could make it much further...

There! Just through the trees up ahead, Zaylie spotted the headlights of an approaching car. She was almost to the road. Suddenly, a vicious growl sounded behind her, and with a gasp, Zaylie dove behind a nearby tree just as the dog lunged at her. It spun around to face her, and through the darkness, she could see its bared teeth glistening in the shadows.

With trembling fingers, Zaylie grasped the can of pepper spray and raised it into the air. Just when the dog was ready to sink its teeth into her flesh, she pressed the trigger and listened as a *whoosh* hissed through the air. The dog jerked back with a howl and began to shake his head, and Zaylie took the chance to make another run for it.

Just then, another pair of headlights appeared to her right, and Zaylie realized Goliath wasn't the only one pursuing her. Alan, it seemed, was also on her trail.

"Has Goliath gotten to you yet?" he called out from his open window.

Ignoring his taunts, Zaylie continued her trek toward the road. Surely, someone would pass by and help her. She could hear Goliath as he wallowed in the leaves behind her, trying to get the burning in his eyes to stop. She almost felt sorry for the poor creature. Almost.

She made it to the road, and judging by the headlights bouncing along Mr. Whitlock's driveway, Alan was almost there as well. She turned and ran in the opposite direction, hoping he wouldn't see her. Suddenly, a car rounded the bend just ahead, and Zaylie began waving her hands frantically, hoping and praying they would stop.

Alan's headlights illuminated Zaylie's figure as she signaled for help, and her heart nearly stopped. The car wasn't slowing down; why wasn't it slowing down?

"Please!" she cried, jumping up and down. "Please, stop!"

Just when she thought the car would pass her by, its tires screeched, and it pulled over onto the shoulder beside her. As Zaylie leaped into her rescuer's car, she saw Alan's headlights click off.

CHAPTER 35

Zaylie

Z aylie, what's going on?"
Looking over at her rescuer, Zaylie realized it was Joan Richards.

"Just drive," she said in a breathless tone. "Hurry!"

Sensing the panic in Zaylie's voice, Joan immediately put her foot on the gas and sped away. As they drove, Zaylie called Sheriff Carter to tell him what happened.

"Miss Layne, you're talking crazy," he stated in disbelief. "Alan Whitlock has always been an upright citizen. Besides, *he* couldn't have killed Azalea."

"I'm telling you the truth, Sheriff," Zaylie insisted. "And I know Alan couldn't have killed Azalea, but his father could have."

Odin sighed. "Okay," he finally said. "If you're filing an official complaint, I'll go pick him up."

After explaining about her car, she asked, "Do you want Joan to drop me at the station?"

"There's no point in your being here right now," he replied. "Just go home and wait until I call you."

When Zaylie hung up, Joan looked at her with wide eyes and said, "I'm in total shock right now.

Are you sure you're okay?"

"Yes, I'm okay," Zaylie replied. With a smile of gratitude, she added, "I wouldn't be, though, if you hadn't come along and stopped to help me. Thank you so much, Joan."

Reaching across the console to pat Zaylie's arm, Joan said, "Of course. After what you did for my grandfather, I'm indebted to you."

"How is he doing, by the way?" Zaylie asked.

Joan pulled her car through the gates at Azalea Bluff and sighed. "He's fading away," she replied, her tone heavy. "It's so hard seeing him like this."

Zaylie nodded sympathetically. She'd lost both of her grandfathers before she was twenty-five, so she knew how badly it hurt.

When Joan pulled up in front of the house, Zaylie thanked her again and jumped out. As she climbed up the porch stairs and Joan drove away, she suddenly felt very alone. The house was still and quiet, and the night was dark. Perhaps she should call Micah and ask him to come stay with her until Odin called.

Zaylie was soon distracted from her thoughts when she entered the house and Smutti came running to greet her.

"Who needs extra company when you're around?" she said with a smile as she leaned over to rub Smutti's back. The dog wiggled around her legs, her pink tongue lolling happily from her mouth.

In the hope of trying to calm herself down,

Zaylie went into the kitchen to fix herself a cup of lavender tea. As the water heated, however, her mind raced. Odin thought she was exaggerating the situation, that much was obvious. There was no way to prove what she said was true, so what would happen when the sheriff questioned the Whitlock men and then let them go? Alan would be back to finish the job, which meant she had to get proof. But how? Suddenly, the last words written in Azalea's diary floated through her mind.

"If you want to know the truth, listen for the sound of the red pecker."

Forgetting all about the tea, Zaylie immediately began searching the house for any sign of a bird or woodpecker. First, she started with the old cuckoo clock in Gran's bedroom; it had belonged to Azalea's mother, and a tiny little bird popped from within the clock each hour. After carefully looking it over, however, Zaylie found nothing. She then went into the living room and searched through the bookshelf. When she came across the book *One Flew Over the Cuckoo's Nest,* her heart nearly stopped. She opened the book and carefully searched through each page, but there was nothing to be found but an old bookmark.

With a sigh, Zaylie replaced the book and slowly walked around the room, deep in thought. When she reached Azalea's portrait, she stopped to stare into the familiar emerald green eyes and wondered what secrets had rested behind that mysterious gaze.

"We used to tell Azalea the red-bellied woodpeckers that would nest in her mother's birdhouses looked like her because of the red hair."

Gran's words suddenly echoed inside Zaylie's mind, and she blinked. Could it be…? Reaching up, Zaylie carefully removed the old painting from the wall and carried it over to the sofa. She turned it away so that the back was facing her and took note of the thick layer of backing board. There were four rickety wooden pins holding it in place, and Zaylie only hoped she wouldn't damage the antique frame in any way.

Taking a deep breath, Zaylie eased the pins away from the backing board. As she carefully pulled the board back, her heart pounded. Why was she so nervous? There was no guarantee that her idea would be correct…

There it was; a large envelope lay nestled in between the painting and the backing board. Zaylie's breath caught. With trembling fingers, she removed the envelope and peered inside to find several sheets of yellowed paper. She pulled the papers from their prison and walked over to the lamp, where she began to read the now familiar handwriting…

I'm writing this letter as I prepare to leave the island for good. I don't know what will become of me, or if I'll even make it, but I've got to try. If something happens to me, however, I want to explain everything in the hope that my friends and family will finally be able to know the whole truth.

When Astrid came to see me earlier today, I discovered who robbed the bank and killed Russell. To my utmost shock, it was Cookie.

"Cookie took the diamonds and shot Russell," she told me, and her words have echoed in my mind all day.

"How do you know this?" I asked her.

Astrid glanced down at her feet, but not before I saw a look of shame on her face. "Because it's what he and I planned all along," she muttered. Looking back up at me, her eyes glistened with tears as she cried, "We never planned for Russell to be killed, though. He heard Cookie opening the safe, and before Cookie could identify himself, Russell shot at him. Cookie shot back, only intending to wound him, but when he realized Russell was dying, he panicked and left."

My eyes narrowing, I asked, "Once again, how do you know all of this?"

Swallowing, Astrid raised her chin and said, "Because we are...were...having an affair. He hates Cynthia and wants to leave her, and those diamonds were going to be our ticket out. We were planning to run away together and disappear."

"So, you're the 'A' my father spoke to about the plane ticket," I said as realization sunk in.

Astrid nodded. "Yes, the airline company called Cookie at the bank about a problem with the reservations, but your father answered instead," she replied. "He was told that I'd booked the tickets, so he came to talk to me."

"What did you tell him?" I wanted to know.

Looking away, Astrid said, "I tried to say it was a surprise trip Cookie was planning for him and Cynthia, but I don't think he believed me."

"Are you also the one who put the note in my purse at Brenda's party?"

Astrid nodded. "Yes," she replied. "I saw you sneaking around outside Cookie's office during the party, listening to his and Harold's conversation. I knew you were poking around too much, and I wanted to frighten you off. I disguised myself and planned to stay in the fort's shadows. I was going to tell you to back off or your family would be in danger, but Toby showed up and I lost my nerve."

"This is incredible," I muttered as I sat back against the sofa's cushion, totally flabbergasted. After a moment, I stated, "You said you **were** having an affair with Cookie. What happened?"

Her jaw clenching slightly, Astrid said, "Cynthia found out about everything, except for me. She knows he was having an affair and planning to run off with someone, but she doesn't know who. She said if he followed through with his plan, she would tell the police everything and they would capture him before he could get out of the country."

"So, she's forcing him to stay with her," I replied, shaking my head in bewilderment. Looking back down at the diamonds in my hand, I asked, "But why give these to me? What am I supposed to do with them?"

Astrid's eyes filled with tears, and she said in a spiteful tone, "Cookie has thrown me aside, and I *refuse to let you pay for his sins. He deserves whatever happens to him."*

Before Zaylie could continue reading, there was a knock on the front door. Hoping it was Odin, Zaylie rushed through the house and into the foyer. She hesitated at the door, however, when the thought crossed her mind that it could be Alan. Leaning forward, she peered through the peephole to see Brenda Cook-Johnson on the other side.

Quickly opening the door, Zaylie ushered her inside and said, "Hello, Mrs. Brenda. Is there something I can do for you?"

"I'm sorry to pop by like this," she replied with a tight smile, "but I was hoping to speak with Louella."

After shutting and locking the front door, Zaylie turned back to face Brenda and said, "I'm sorry, but she's not here. She's staying the night with a sick friend. Is there anything I can help you with?"

Her eyes drifting down to the old letter that Zaylie still held in her hand, she asked, "What do you have there?"

Zaylie's heart quickened. How had she forgotten to leave the letter in the living room? She couldn't show Brenda, not with the accusations the letter held about her father.

Quickly tucking the letter behind her back, Zaylie shrugged innocently and said, "Oh, it's nothing for you to bother with." Clearing her throat, she stepped around Brenda and asked,

"Would you like something to drink?"

When Brenda didn't immediately answer, Zaylie turned around to find that the older woman had pulled something from her purse and was pointing it directly at Zaylie.

She was holding a gun.

CHAPTER 36

Zaylie

What are you doing?" Zaylie asked, her eyes widening in shock.

"Hand it over," Brenda replied coolly.

"Hand *what* over?" Zaylie wanted to know.

"The diary, and whatever *that* is," she stated, pointing to the letter.

Zaylie eyed the gun in Brenda's hand, her mind racing. She could easily overpower the older woman, but getting the upper hand could be tricky, especially if Brenda was very good with a gun.

"Brenda, what is this all about?" Zaylie asked, hoping to distract the woman while she figured out what to do.

"I don't have time to dawdle," Brenda snapped, raising the gun higher. "Just give me what I've asked for, and no one has to get hurt."

Her eyes narrowing, Zaylie said in a cool tone, "I'll give you this letter, but I won't give you the diary and you won't be able to find it on your own. Tell me what's going on first, and then we'll see about the diary."

Brenda studied Zaylie for a moment, as if trying to determine how serious she was. Finally, she held out her hand and said, "Give me the letter first."

Zaylie did as she was told. Just as Brenda's fingers touched the old, yellowed paper, Zaylie was ready to make her move. Before she could follow through, however, Smutti appeared in the doorway and let out a fierce bark.

Brenda jerked the gun in the dog's direction, and Zaylie's heart nearly stopped. "Here, take the letter," she cried, trying to bring Brenda's attention back to her.

Brenda didn't fail to notice the panic in Zaylie's voice. Snatching the letter, she said in a steely tone, "Now give me the diary or I'll shoot the dog."

Zaylie could see that she meant it, so she told Smutti to "stay" and then began walking upstairs. Brenda followed, and while they walked, everything slowly started to click together in Zaylie's mind.

"Alan called and told you what happened tonight," she stated matter-of-factly. "The two of you are in this together, aren't you?"

When Brenda didn't answer, Zaylie stopped on the second from the top stair and turned to look at her. "Aren't you?" she asked more forcefully.

"I never planned for him to kill you," Brenda replied. "He was simply supposed to get the diary and that was it, but he got greedy."

Zaylie studied the woman's faded, wrinkled eyes. "How did you know what your father did?" she asked.

Brenda's jaw tightened, but she didn't say a word. As her thoughts kept making more and more sense, Zaylie kept talking.

"Did J.R. tell you after he overheard Azalea and Astrid's conversation?" she pressed. When Brenda glanced away, Zaylie's eyes widened and she asked in a shocked whisper, "Were *you* the one who came back to the house that night and killed Azalea?"

Jerking her gaze back to Zaylie, the older woman raised the gun and hissed, "You can't prove anything, young lady, and you won't force a confession out of me. Now get that diary before my patience runs out!"

Zaylie turned and took the final step that led to the upper floor. She went into her room, slipped the chain that held the key from around her neck and unlocked the writing desk. She then did exactly as she had before to find the compartment that hid Azalea's diary. She could feel Brenda's eyes boring into her, and when she turned to give her the diary, Brenda's lip had curled into a victorious smirk.

"I'll have to tell Sheriff Carter about this," Zaylie said as she handed the book to Brenda. "Or are you planning to kill me like you killed Azalea?"

Brenda took the diary and said, "I don't want to hurt you, Zaylie. If you don't keep your mouth shut about this, though, I have people who can do what needs to be done."

"People like Alan?" Zaylie raised her eyebrows.

"People who will do whatever I say for a little

bit of money," Brenda replied. "So, before you spread the rumors from this diary, you'd better first think about yourself, your dog, and even your grandmother."

Zaylie felt the blood leave her face at Brenda's words. Ever since Brenda pulled out that gun and stated her reasons for being there, Zaylie had planned to overpower her at some point and tell Odin what happened. Brenda was, however, just a little old lady...or so Zaylie had thought. She hadn't considered the power this woman evidently had, nor had she taken into account the danger her loved ones may be in if she shared the contents of Azalea's diary and letter.

"You'd go that far to protect your family's reputation?" Zaylie asked in a choked whisper.

Brenda raised a cool eyebrow. "You can count on it."

With those words, she spun around and hurried downstairs. Zaylie considered going after her, but was it worth it? She had no proof that Brenda came to the house, pulled a gun on her, and stole their property. By the time Odin could get a search warrant, Brenda would have already destroyed the diary and the letter.

"I can't believe I'm doing this," Zaylie muttered to herself. "Am I really going to let this woman intimidate me and get away with this?"

No, she was not. Brenda may try to harm her family, but Zaylie knew people who could help protect them. She wasn't about to back down from this fight.

Squaring her shoulders, Zaylie marched from the room and hurried down the stairs after Brenda. The older woman had already made it to the bottom floor, and when she heard Zaylie coming, she spun around with the gun. Smutti stood in the living room doorway, watching the scene with a guarded stance.

"You won't get away with this, Brenda," Zaylie cried. "Gran and I will tell Uncle Bill and Odin everything that Azalea wrote; your family's name will be mud once we're through. Unless that is, you give me back the diary and letter and turn yourself in for the things you've done."

Brenda's faded eyes had turned steely, and she firmly shook her head. "No," she stated in a deadly tone. Raising the gun higher, she added, "You're just like Azalea. I guess I'll have to kill you now, just like I did her."

Brenda's finger was over the trigger when Zaylie signaled to Smutti with a flick of her hand. In one split second, the dog lunged across the room and dove toward Brenda. The gun fired, and Zaylie dropped to the stairs with a scream as she covered her head.

In those few heart-pounding seconds, a million thoughts raced through Zaylie's head. Was Smutti dead? Had Brenda shot her? What if Brenda was dead and Zaylie had to try to explain everything to Odin?

Suddenly, there came a pounding at the front

door. Trembling all over, Zaylie raised her head to find Brenda lying on the floor with blood oozing from her head. Smutti stood over the woman, her teeth bared as she guarded the enemy. Standing, Zaylie hurried down the stairs and picked up the gun.

"Miss Layne?" Sheriff Carter's voice called out from the front porch. "Are you in there? Open up!"

With a feeling of relief, Zaylie hurried to the door. Before she swung it open, she paused and glanced back. Making a last-minute decision, she grabbed Azalea's letter and tucked it into her pocket. She wanted to finish reading it before handing it over to the police.

When Zaylie threw open the door, Odin blinked in surprise when he spotted the gun in her hand, and then he noticed Brenda lying on the floor behind her. Glancing down at the gun, Zaylie's heart sank. Why had she picked it up? Now Odin would never believe her.

"This isn't what it looks like, Sheriff," she began in a trembling voice.

Raising a hand, Odin nodded and said, "I know. J.R. just told us everything."

Tilting her head to the side, Zaylie asked, "What do you mean?"

"He followed Brenda that night," he replied in a grave tone. "He knows she killed Azalea."

CHAPTER 37

Zaylie

Her eyes widening in shock at the sheriff's words, Zaylie asked, "Why did he keep it to himself all these years?"

Beckoning for Zaylie to follow him outside while his men went into the house to see about Brenda, Odin said, "He refuses to say. I think it has something to do with the diamonds, but we may never know. Alan won't admit to doing anything wrong, but I have a feeling that Brenda will rat him out, which is probably why J.R. finally told on her."

Zaylie shook her head in disbelief. "I can't believe this," she stated as she reached down to rub Smutti's back. "I don't understand, though, why Brenda killed Azalea. What was the point?"

"She was afraid Azalea would tell her father's secret," Odin replied. "Brenda was very close to her mother, and I think she did it to protect her from the shame and stigma that comes with being a scorned wife."

Why not kill Astrid, too? Zaylie wondered, and then she remembered what Azalea had written. Astrid had washed her hands of the whole ordeal and wanted nothing more to do with it. She even wondered if Brenda had threatened the girl, therefore ensuring her silence. If she'd only known that Azalea had planned to leave the island for good, she wouldn't have had a reason to kill her.

The front door opened then, and two policemen walked out with Brenda, one on either side of her. Her head was still bleeding, but her eyes were fiery and filled with hate as she glared at Zaylie. It was at that moment that Zaylie knew yet another reason Brenda had killed Azalea: she'd secretly despised her.

Zaylie went down to the station that night and gave a full statement. She called Gran and told her what happened, and when Gran said she would leave Jan and come back home, Zaylie insisted she stay with her friend.

"Everyone is behind bars," she assured her nearly frantic grandmother. "I'll be fine. I promise. I may even go stay with Rita tonight."

After getting Gran to calm down, Zaylie left the station and called Rita. She was just as upset as Gran when Zaylie explained the details of the night and insisted she come over to spend the night.

"It would be way too creepy to stay at that place tonight after everything that's happened," Rita stated, and Zaylie could picture her friend shuddering dramatically.

Zaylie agreed, and after going home to gather Smutti and quickly pack an overnight bag, she headed over to her friend's house. When she arrived, she was surprised to find that Ryker was there, too.

"Here to crash the party?" she asked him teasingly.

Ryker grinned. "I always make parties better, not worse," he replied as he took Zaylie's bag inside for her.

"He was here fixing my kitchen sink when you called," Rita explained as she hurried to her friend's side. Throwing her arms around Zaylie's neck, she cried, "I'm so glad you're okay!"

They all went into the kitchen, which smelled like freshly baked cookies. "When you agreed to come over, I made chocolate chip cookies," Rita said with a wide smile as she hurried over to the oven to remove the treat. "When I was on Broadway, I couldn't eat like this."

"Better watch it, sis, or you'll get pudgy," Ryker teased.

Spinning around to face her brother, Rita's eyes were already filling with tears as she asked, "Am I seriously getting fat? I've never owned a pair of scales before, so tell me the truth!"

Rolling his eyes, Ryker stated, "No, you're not getting fat. Now hurry up and get those cookies out of the oven before they burn."

Laughing at the familiar camaraderie between the twins, Zaylie grabbed a soft drink from the fridge and sat at the kitchen table. As they ate the delicious cookies, they talked about the Whitlocks and Brenda and the whole sordid mess.

"Who knew so much drama existed on our tiny little island?" Rita said as she licked chocolate from her fingers.

They continued to talk, and after a while, they decided to play a game of Monopoly. It lasted for nearly three hours, with Zaylie and Ryker both beating out Rita. With a yawn, Rita announced that she was going to bed.

"You know where the guest room is," Rita said as she hugged Zaylie. "Good night, you two. And Zaylie? Please make sure you beat him; he thinks he always has to win this game."

Smiling, Zaylie quipped, "He thinks he has to win at *everything*."

"Hey, I can't help that I'm good at most things," Ryker replied, his eyes twinkling.

The game lasted another hour, and if Rita hadn't been in bed, Zaylie would have shouted for joy when Ryker finally admitted defeat.

"You're the only female I've ever let win," he stated as he put the game away.

"*Let*?" Zaylie asked with a laugh. "I won fair and square and you know it."

Sitting back at the table across from her, Ryker said, "Okay, fine. I'll get you next time." Leaning his elbows onto the table, he eyed her for a moment before saying, "I heard you and Micah are back together."

Zaylie blinked at the sudden change in subject. "Oh, uh, yes. Yes, we are," she stammered.

"He's a lucky guy," Ryker said. He took a sip of

tea, his eyes intense as he studied her over the rim. Placing the glass back on the table, he stated, "I guess I should have swept you off your feet before he had the chance."

Uncertain whether he was joking or not, Zaylie smirked and said, "I'm sure your girlfriend would be happy to share you."

Tilting his head to the side, Ryker asked, "Why do you keep saying I have a girlfriend?"

"I heard you were dating some girl you met in Savannah," Zaylie replied with a shrug.

With a laugh, Ryker shook his head and said, "You must be talking about Sarah. She and I aren't dating; we met when I was in the military. She's engaged to one of my best friends."

Zaylie blinked. "Oh…I see," she replied, feeling a little embarrassed that he now knew she listened to the rumor mill.

"Were you jealous?" he asked with a grin.

Rolling her eyes, Zaylie stated drolly, "More like I felt sorry for the poor girl."

Ryker smiled and stood up. He walked over to where Zaylie sat and leaned down until their faces were only inches apart. Zaylie swallowed past the sudden lump in her throat and tried to ignore the hot flush that swept over her body.

"Just remember that Pierce didn't get your first kiss; I did," Ryker stated in a low, husky tone.

As he stood up and sauntered out the front door, Zaylie called out, "If it's not voluntarily given, it doesn't count."

She could hear Ryker's laughter as he left the house, and she shook her head. As she cleaned up the kitchen and headed to the guest bedroom, Zaylie wondered why that man insisted on being so annoying.

As Zaylie was changing her clothes and getting ready for bed, she suddenly remembered that Azalea's letter was still tucked away in her sweater pocket. She pulled the folded, yellowed papers out and stared at them, wondering if she dared read them without Gran.

I've already read the first page, she thought as she sat down on the bed. *I might as well read the rest.*

Carefully unfolding the letter, Zaylie picked up where she'd left off in Azalea's final words.

Now that you know about Astrid and what I plan to do tonight, I feel there's something else that I must confess. The night Russell was killed, we weren't simply going to elope. We were planning to steal the diamonds first. It was wrong of us, I know, but I was desperate to get out of Papa's house and away from Whisper Island. I need freedom; I need a change. I've felt like a prisoner ever since Papa refused to let me marry Russell, and this seemed to be the only way to finally get free...and perhaps it was also my way of getting back at Papa. Russell and I were going to take the diamonds and disappear forever, but Cookie beat us to it. I suppose I'll always hate him for that.

Zaylie lowered the letter, her face ashen. How

could Azalea have planned to do something so terrible to her friends and family? And how could Gran have been so fooled by her best friend?

Gran. She would be heartbroken if she knew about this. Standing, Zaylie hurried over to her suitcase and tucked the letter underneath her clothes. Maybe she would tell Gran, and maybe she wouldn't. She'd think about it and decide later.

As Zaylie went into the bathroom to wash her face and brush her teeth, a question suddenly flashed across her mind. Whatever happened to the diamonds? Did Brenda take them? Or J.R.? Or perhaps Azalea hid them before Brenda killed her.

Or perhaps they would never know what really happened to those diamonds.

A NOTE FROM THE AUTHOR

Thank you so much for reading "Killer Pursuit". If you enjoyed it, please leave a review on Amazon or Goodreads – or both! Reviews really help! I look forward to hearing from you. If you're interested in receiving news of upcoming books, discounts, free e-books and more, please sign up for my newsletter at:

https://newsletter.jennyelaineauthor.com/

Also, don't forget to check out my other books at:

https://jennyelaineauthor.com/

Made in the USA
Monee, IL
05 November 2024

69413310R00163